SAMMY FERAL'S
DIARIES
of
WEiRD
YETI RESCUE

Books by Eleanor Hawken

Sammy Feral's Diaries of Weird

Sammy Feral's Diaries of Weird: Yeti Rescue

SAMMY FERAL'S DIARIES OF WEIRD

YETI RESCUE

Eleanor Hawken

Illustrations by John Kelly

Quercus

ACKNOWLEDGEMENTS

Huge thanks to everyone who helps make my dreams come true by being part of Team Sammy Feral. Thank you to Sarah Lambert, Alice Hill, Niamh Mulvey and everyone else at Quercus Children's Books. Thanks to John Kelly for once again providing such fantastic illustrations, my agent Victoria Birkett, my husband Luke Willis and to both the Hawken and Willis families for all their love and support. And thank YOU for reading about Sammy's weird adventures . . . I hope you enjoy reading the book as much as I enjoyed writing it!

First published in Great Britain in 2012 by

Quercus
55 Baker Street
7th Floor, South Block
London
W1U 8EW

A CIP catalogue record for this book is available from the British Library

ISBN 978 1 78206 189 2

1 3 5 7 9 10 8 6 4 2

For my father, who introduced me to

the Jabberwocky —

to this day my favourite weird animal

Thursday 25th June

The Feral Scale of Weirdness shot right through the roof today. In fact, it shot through the roof, blasted up through the Earth's atmosphere, orbited the sun and then whizzed into hyper-space. My world is weird, weird, weird . . .

Just when I thought life was getting back to normal, well, as normal as life can be when these are the people I see every day:

1

MY FAMILY
Mum and Dad
My sisters, Grace and Natty
Caliban, our ex-werewolf dog

✱ All ex-werewolves (thanks to Caliban).

✱ Still have excessive ear hair and an annoyingly good sense of smell.

✱ Whatever you do, don't get in their way during the full moon. They still get seriously tetchy!

DONNY

* A world-famous cryptozoologist – that's someone who studies animals which supposedly don't exist.

* Has grey hair and crazy clothes.

* Pets include a fire-breathing turtle, a phoenix and a three-headed gut worm.

RED

* Moody emo-teen supreme.

* Has the power of telekinesis (she can move things with her mind. How cool is that!)

* Serious sense of humour bypass.

Since they helped me cure my family of the werewolf virus, Donny and Red have lived at Feral Zoo. Weird is right up their street, and they know just what to do when things turn a little crazy. So it's always good to have them around on days like today.

As well as being ex-werewolves, my family also owns Feral Zoo. Feral Zoo is the only interesting thing about the town of Tyler's Rest, and I help out there most evenings and week-ends. Spending all my free time in the zoo is pretty sweet. Take last week, for example – I've been perfecting a recipe for the best Komodo dragon-feed known to man. A mixture of newt legs, pigs' ears and prune juice works a treat with those grouchy bad-breath mega-lizards.

Earlier, I was on my way to the reptile house to hang out with my pet python Beelzebub when I heard a strange noise. It was a cross between a hissing snake, a man speaking Russian and my younger sister Natty when she hasn't had her daily feed of raw sausages. The sound was coming from Backstage – the part of the zoo that's shut off to visitors – the part of the zoo where Donny and Red live.

I decided to check it out. As I got closer to Backstage – passing the elephants and Darwin the gorilla on the way – the noise got louder. Not only louder but clearer. Suddenly it was less like a noise and more like a voice. The voice sounded scared, terrified, like it was fighting for its life. I started to run . . . and panic . . . This wouldn't be the first time I'd found myself in a life-or-death situation!

I arrived at the Backstage gates. Suddenly the voice was crystal clear.

'Please – I need help!' it screamed in terror. *'I'm not here to hurt anyone! Please! Please!'*

I barged through the gate and slammed it behind me. No way did I want the regular zoo visitors witnessing wacko-time Backstage. That's when I saw them – Donny and Red fighting what can only be described as a giant worm.

Worm the size of a Labrador = level 1 on the Feral Scale of Weirdness!

'Get back, Sammy!' Donny screamed at me as he whipped a lasso above his head before tossing it at the giant worm. As the rope caught around the worm's thick body, it hissed in anger and spat bright yellow venom at Donny. The worm's spit missed my friend and sizzled where it hit the ground.

'It spits acid!' Red yelled. My jaw dropped open like a lion devouring

a wildebeest! I watched as Red tore off a piece of metal from the fence with nothing but the power of her mind. She forced the metal down on to the ground and used it as a shield to bat away the acidic spit that flew from the giant worm's fangs.

'Whatever you do,' Donny shouted at me, 'don't stare it in the eye. One look from his eyes means instant death!'

Err, rewind!

What kind of animal spits acid and can kill you with a look?

'What is it?' I screamed back, panicking and covering my eyes with my hands. I've lived though way too much weirdness to be killed by just a look – from a worm! I stumbled backwards, desperate to get away from the acid-spitting freak-worm.

'It's a Mongolian death worm!' Donny and Red shouted in unison.

Mongolian death worms = extremely bad news!

I've read about the Mongolian death worm before in one of Donny's cryptozoology books.

The Mongolian Death Worm

Looks like: Giant worm the size of a large dog. Pink body. Small eyes. Fangs as sharp as daggers.

Natural habitat: The deserts of Outer Mongolia.

Deadly features: Spits acid. Can kill you with a stare.

Best methods of defence: NEVER look it in the eye. Wear acid-proof clothing. Avoid the deserts of Outer Mongolia.

'Here!' Donny screamed to Red, throwing her the rope end and tightening it around the worm's writhing body. That's when I noticed something — the worm was wearing a back-pack!

What's weirder than a Mongolian death worm? A Mongolian death worm wearing a backpack! Was it planning to stay?

Red took the rope from Donny and held it firm as Donny pulled out his tranquillizing blowpipe from his pocket. He put the pipe to his lips and prepared to strike.

'Please, no!' came the strange voice I'd heard outside the gates only moments earlier. *'I mean you no harm!'*

'WAIT!' I screamed. 'Don't shoot!'

Donny stared at me as though I'd just told him I fancied a cuddle with the death worm.

'Don't shoot!' I repeated. Stumbling forward, careful not to look the worm in the eye, I raised my hands in surrender. *'Don't spit at me!'* I warned the worm.

'Tell your friend not to shoot and you have my word,' the death worm replied.

I should probably mention at this point

that I have powers of CSC. That means I'm a Cross-Species Communicator. I can speak the languages of animals – not regular animals like dogs and cats, only rare animals. I can understand animals like werewolves, phoenixes and Mongolian death worms, when no one else can. It's pretty cool.

'It's not here to hurt you,' I told Donny and Red.

'Funny way of showing it,' grunted Red angrily. Red loves any excuse to grunt. In fact, I've known warthogs who are better company than Red. 'Tell the worm to quit with the acid if he wants to talk.'

The worm let out a horrible hiss. *'Who is this freak?'* I heard it say.

'This is Red,' I answered back. *'She lives here. So does Donny. Is it Donny you're here to see?'* As Donny is a world-famous cryptozoologist, if there's a Mongolian death worm hanging around

Feral Zoo, it kind of figures that it's here because of him.

'Who's Donny?' the worm asked.

'What's it saying?' Donny asked.

'It doesn't know who you are,' I told him, 'but it says it's here because it needs help.'

Donny frowned. 'Ask its name.'

'My name is Genghis,' the death worm replied, without waiting for me to translate.

'Like Genghis Khan?' I gasped. We learned about the famous Mongolian warrior at school. He was mega-fierce, just like the death worm now standing in front of me.

'Yes,' Genghis answered. *'My best friend has gone missing,'* he continued slowly, as if he was weighing up whether to trust me or not. *'Coming to Feral Zoo was my last hope of finding him.'*

'Who's your friend?' I asked quickly.

'Bert, the Chief of the Yetis,' he hissed. *'He and I go way back. The Tibetan plains, the deserts of*

11

Mongolia, the mountains of Nepal — we've seen it all. Man, he and I have had some wild times. I could tell you some stories . . . ever seen a yak fire a rocket from its nostril?'

'What's it saying?' Donny asked.

I shook my head. 'Something about a Yeti Chief and watching yaks fire rockets from their nostrils.'

'You know Bert?' Donny asked the worm, careful not to look it in the eye.

'You know Bert?' I asked Donny in amazement. Although why I should be surprised that Donny knows the Yeti Chief and rocket-firing yaks, I don't know. Stuff like that is as normal as brushing your teeth to Donny.

Genghis growled. I could sense he didn't like being interrupted mid-story. Who would have thought that Mongolian death worms are such dreadful attention seekers, huh?

'Bert and I were heading over here on holiday,'

Genghis explained. *'We just wanted to get away from the mountains for a while. See some of the world. We stowed away on a ship to cross the ocean . . .*

'We were meant to reconvene up on deck at sunset. Kick back and watch the waves roll across the horizon. But Bert never came. I searched that ship high and low, but he was nowhere to be found. Back on dry land I continued to search for him. Bert has spent his life

helping others, including me, I can't just give up on him. I've looked everywhere, spoken to everyone — no sign. He's literally vanished into thin air.'

'How does a yeti vanish into thin air?' I wondered aloud. 'Aren't those things as large as a house?'

'Bert's not the kind of yeti to just do a vanishing act,' Donny said, scratching his head of grey hair in thought. 'If he's gone missing, then something is definitely up.'

'How do we go about finding a missing yeti?' Red asked. 'And if the death worm doesn't want our help, then why is it here at Feral Zoo?'

Genghis tutted in frustration. *'There's something else: a letter arrived at my wormhole a couple of days ago. A ransom note.'*

'A ransom note?!' I said in horror. 'Bert's been kidnapped?'

'The note's in there.' Genghis nodded towards his backpack.

14

'The very latest in Mongolian-death-worm fashion,' Red teased, as she nervously edged towards the bag, flipped it open and pulled out a scrunched-up piece of paper.

Red tossed me the note. 'You read it, kid. I need to keep my eye on Mr Poison-Spit.'

The ransom note was pieced together from letters cut out of newspapers and magazines.

Dear Genghis,
I have your friend Bert, the Yeti Chief. I'm holding him captive somewhere you will never find him.
If you ever want to see Bert again then you'll need to find the wish frog. He is your only hope.
Yours faithfully,
Your worst nightmare.

There was a clump of sandy-coloured hair taped to the letter. *'Yeti fur,'* Genghis confirmed.

Donny took the note from my hands and carefully peeled the hair from the page. 'I'll take this to the lab to verify it's genuine.'

'So now you know why I'm here.' Genghis shrugged. *'To ask the wish frog for help.'*

Most people might wonder what a wish frog is. But not me. I've read all about them in Donny's Cryptozoology books. Three guesses what a wish frog can do . . .

'A wish frog?' I gasped. 'Here at Feral Zoo?'

'No way,' Donny shook his head. 'Wish

frogs are extinct. The last wish frog went into retirement years ago. He must be long dead by now. There's no way he's here at Feral Zoo. Whoever sent Genghis to find the frog has sent him off on a wild goose chase.'

'Wake up and smell the frogspawn, Donny!' Genghis said impatiently. *'The last wish frog is alive and kicking, and has been living at Feral Zoo for years. It's the perfect hideout.'* Every time I heard Genghis's voice I had to remember not to look him in the eye.

I shook my head in amazement. 'A wish frog here – at Feral Zoo? Can my day get any stranger?'

'Only one way to find out.' Red shrugged, raising a heavily painted eyebrow.

'Let's go check out the amphibian house.' Donny nodded in understanding.

'What about me?' Genghis asked, squirming in the rope that sat tight around his body.

'You're staying right where you are,' I replied, speaking in Death Worm. 'There's no way I'm letting a Mongolian death worm wriggle around the zoo.'

Red tied the rope holding Genghis to the fence, securing him safely. 'Taking no chances,' she grumbled.

'You have to take me!' Genghis wriggled his fat body in frustration. 'You think you're so smart, but the wish frog's been hiding under your nose for years. You don't even know what he looks like!'

The death worm had a point. I can tell the difference between dozens of frog species – but a wish frog? I wouldn't know what a wish frog looked like if it hopped on to my face and danced the cancan.

'We need him.' I shrugged at Donny. 'He's the only one who can recognise the wish frog.'

'So we wait.' Donny sighed. 'When the visitors have left the zoo then we'll take him with us.'

That was a couple of hours ago. I've been writing in my diary since then. It's important to document these things – what if I'm killed by death-worm venom this evening? Who would tell my strange story then?

We're heading to the amphibian house now. I'll report back as soon as I can.

Mongolian death worms, missing Yeti Chiefs and retired wish frogs. Weird by anyone's standards . . . right?

8 P.M.

As soon as the zoo gates were locked and the last visitor had gone, we left Backstage. I led the way, Donny, Red and Genghis following closely behind.

'Keep your eyes to the ground and your

fangs in your mouth,' I heard Donny say sternly to Genghis.

'Jeez,' Genghis said bitterly. *'It's as if you think I don't know how to act around people. This isn't the first time I've had to grit my fangs and put up with humans.'*

'You understand English?' I asked Genghis, realising he knew what Donny had said.

'Sure,' he replied. *'I can read it too. It's hardly complicated. I've just never learned to speak it. English isn't exactly a useful language anyway. Not like Yeti — I spent years learning to speak that. But English . . . what's the point? I guess it's lucky I have you here to translate.'*

Backstage isn't far from the amphibian house — we only had to pass the Galapagos tortoises and the Komodo dragons and we were there. The Feral Zoo amphibian house is home to hundreds of salamanders, toads and frogs. Genghis led the way past tanks of poison-dart frogs, rocket frogs and the largest frog known to man – the Goliath frog.

'So which one is he?' Donny asked, peering into the tank of a strawberry dart frog.

I looked over Donny's shoulder and stared suspiciously at a multicoloured tree frog. If a frog is able to grant wishes, it must look pretty special. Genghis writhed towards the back of the room, where we keep the horned frogs. *'He's over here,'* he hissed back at us.

The wish frog = a horned frog?

I did not see that one coming!

Let me just explain a few things about horned frogs:

* They're mega-lazy – they sit around all day waiting for prey to just walk by.

* They're mega-greedy – they'll eat anything, even if they suffocate themselves in the process.

* They're mega-aggressive — nothing scares them.

* They're mega-ugly — spiky horns and a massive mouth.

I walked over to the horned-frog tank and peered in. There was one particularly fat frog in there. His eyes were closed and his tongue lolled lazily out of the side of his mouth. I tapped on the glass.

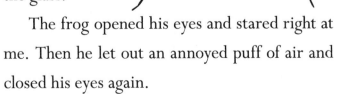

The frog opened his eyes and stared right at me. Then he let out an annoyed puff of air and closed his eyes again.

'Lift me up!' Genghis squirmed at my feet.

Er, no way am I picking up a Mongolian death worm any time soon, sorry!

Donny looked down at Genghis and sighed. 'I'll pick him up.' He scooped up the worm's fat body and lifted him up to the glass window. I tapped on the glass again. The frog only scrunched his eyes tighter in annoyance.

'Tap again,' Genghis instructed.

'Hey!' I tapped.

'Wish Frog!' Genghis whispered.

Nothing.

'Wish Frog!' he said a little louder. Still nothing. *'WISH FROG!!!!'* He screamed so loudly the window shook and acidic spit scorched the glass. The frog's bulging eyes popped open in horror and he stared straight at the worm.

'Genghis?' the frog croaked.

'Yep.' I nodded over to Donny. 'That's no normal frog. I just heard it speak.'

Wish Frog

Looks like: Horned Frog

Natural habitat: The Amazon Rainforest

Amazing abilities: Can grant wishes

Freaky fact: Believed by cryptozoologists to be extinct – turns out we have the last living wish frog at Feral Zoo

Donny put Genghis down on the ground and I opened up the frog's tank. I reached in and picked the bullish frog up. His thick legs kicked in protest. *'It's OK,'* I reassured him. *'I work here, remember?'*

'Since when can you speak Wish Frog?' the frog asked. 'You don't need to bother – I've been hopping about long enough to learn English. I also speak Mongolian Death Worm. *Hello, Genghis – how are you?'* He narrowed his eyes in thought and muttered, *'And what were you thinking by bringing humans to me? Do I need to remind you that you took a vow of secrecy?'*

'I know there are only a few of us in the world who know your true location,' Genghis said apologetically, 'and that we've all sworn to protect you. And I know I vowed to never come looking for you except in an absolute emergency.'

'This is amazing!' Donny beamed with delight, speaking over Genghis. 'All this time, the last remaining wish frog has been here – in Feral Zoo! Let me introduce myself – I'm Donny. And your name is . . . ?'

'I don't need a name – I'm the last of my kind. You can call me Wish Frog. And listen, dude,' the frog said sleepily, sitting back in the palm of my hand, 'I don't want any trouble. I'm living the easy life here at Feral Zoo. All I'm interested in is free food and the pretty tree frog in the tank opposite.'

'Well, get ready to hop right out of retirement,' said Genghis. 'I need your help.'

The frog rolled his bulging eyes. 'You know

as well as I do, Worm, I'm out of the wish-granting game for good.'

'Well, you need to get back to work. Bert's been kidnapped!'

The frog lifted his horned eyebrows in surprise. 'Bert – the Yeti Chief? Kidnapped?'

I pulled the ransom note from my pocket and waved it in front of him. 'The only way we can rescue Bert is with your help.'

The wish frog leaned forward and studied the ransom note carefully. A look of utter horror filled his little face. *'Genghis, what have you done? You've . . . you've led the kidnapper straight to me!'*

I looked around, almost expecting the kidnapper to jump around the corner and surprise us. But there was no one there. I had no idea what the wish frog was talking about.

'You, Genghis, are one of the only creatures in this entire world who knows where I am!'

Wow, the wish frog sounded mega-angry.

'Do I need to remind you why I went into hiding in the first place? There are a lot of very greedy, evil people out there who'd like to get their hands on me and force me to grant their wishes. People who would stop at nothing to find me. Even kidnap a Yeti Chief!'

Genghis gulped loudly. 'I didn't think of that,' he muttered.

'Do you ever think, Genghis?' The wish frog rolled his eyes in despair.

'*But now I'm here,*' Genghis pleaded, '*you could grant me a wish and bring Bert home safely.*'

'Oh no, no way!' the frog croaked in English. 'Just about every war, natural disaster and major sporting defeat of the last century was because of a wish gone wrong. Trust me, granting wishes is bad news.' He looked at Genghis thoughtfully and a flicker of sadness ran through his eyes. 'But Bert . . . kidnapped? We've been friends for decades. He's been a hairy shoulder to cry on every time a wish went wrong. He's so strong, so dependable!'

'There aren't that many creatures strong enough to overpower a yeti,' said Donny, shaking his head solemnly. 'But at least we now know the motive behind the kidnap – to find the wish frog. And if Genghis has already led them to Feral Zoo, it's only a matter of time before the kidnapper makes their next move. This really is bad news.'

Bad news = not what I want to hear!

'OK, I'll help you,' the frog said slowly.

Woo hoo!!

'You'll grant us a wish and find Bert?' I grinned widely.

'No way.' He shook his head. 'No wishes granted – ever. But I'll help you, in any other way I can.'

'Well, that's better than nothing, I guess.' Donny shrugged. 'We'll set up a tank for you Backstage and you can live with us while we track down Bert.'

What a day in the life of Sammy Feral! The case of the missing yeti is officially open. A crack team has been assembled. The stakes are high . . . and the heat is on!

Friday 26th June

The person who invented school clearly had nothing better to do than sit in a stuffy classroom being bored all day. I have a gazillion better things to do – like getting to the bottom of who's after the wish frog and rescue Bert the Yeti Chief!

I came home from a dull day to find Mum waiting for me in the kitchen. She had two things to give me.

'A ham sandwich, Sammy.' She smiled and passed me my favourite after-school snack. 'And this book from Donny.'

A Beginner's Guide to Yetis.

'He said you need to brush up on your yeti knowledge,' Mum said, folding her arms and eyeing me with suspicion. 'Should I be worried?'

Because my family used to be werewolves, they're pretty clued up when it comes to weird animals. Most mums would think nothing of their kid reading a book about yetis, but my mum knows better. She knows that yetis exist and that I'm more than likely going to meet one, some day.

'It's OK,' I assured her through a mouthful of sandwich. 'Everything's under control.'

'Just don't let it get in the way of your homework,' Mum said sternly.

Geez! Only Mum would think that homework was more important than yetis!

I've spent the evening reading the yeti book. Homework can wait. I now know enough about yetis to write my own book:

Sammy Feral's Guide
to Yetis

Chapter I
An Introduction to Yetis

* Yetis are nearly three metres tall and are covered in shaggy golden fur

* They are vegetarian (surprisingly)

* These big-footed beasts can kill with a single swipe of their powerful paw

* Yetis are native to the mountains of Nepal in Asia, although they have lived in other parts of the world for thousands of years

* They can communicate with each other across vast distances – they do this by putting out the Call of the Yeti

I also tried to do some research on wish frogs this evening. But the Internet came up with a big fat nothing. It turns out that wish frogs are so mythical there aren't even any myths about them!

Saturday 27th June

Saturday = zoo time!

All I wanted to do today was rush Backstage and check in with the Crypto Gang. But even I have responsibilities that have to come before rescuing yetis. Today's jobs included feeding the meerkats, cleaning out the gibbon enclosure and reinforcing the warthogs' fence. I managed to get all of that done before lunchtime, so I made my way towards Backstage, eating a sandwich as I walked.

'I hope you washed your hands?' I heard Mum say as she poked her head out of the bearded-pig enclosure. Natty popped up beside

Mum with what looked like a handful of pig feed in her tiny palms.

'Er, shouldn't you be worrying about what Natty's eating, Mum?' I pointed out. 'At least the sight of me munching on a sandwich won't make people suspicious.'

Mum knocked the food out of Natty's hand, 'How many times do I have to tell you, Natty, not at the zoo! You can eat whatever you want at home, but . . .'

'But, Mum, I'm hungry!' Natty wailed, stamping her feet. A bearded pig grunted at Natty and waddled away in fright.

'Sammy –' Mum came closer to me as I popped the last bit of sandwich crust into my mouth – 'have you upset Grace?'

'No more than usual.' I shrugged.

'She's been acting very strangely recently,' Mum said with concern. 'She won't tell me what's wrong.'

'I heard her shouting at Max this morning,' Natty added self-importantly. Max is Grace's boyfriend and one of the junior zookeepers here at Feral Zoo. Natty likes to think she knows everything, even though she's only six years old. 'And he shouted back at her.'

'I wonder what could be wrong,' Mum muttered. 'If you find anything out, Sammy, let me know, please.'

'Trust me, Mum,' I said, beginning to walk away. 'I'd rather sit in the vulture enclosure with meat tied around my neck than get in the way of Grace when she's in one of her moods!'

I let myself in Backstage and headed straight for the offices. There are two small rooms and a kitchen and a bathroom in there. It's where Donny and Red live and where they keep their pets.

Red was reading a book about Nepal, Donny was cleaning out the phoenix's ashes, Genghis

was kicking back by the gut worm's tank and the wish frog was sleeping in the kitchen sink.

Nothing strange here then!

'What took you so long?' Donny said, sounding annoyed. 'I thought you were gonna get here first thing?'

'Nice to see you too.' I smiled. 'I came as quickly as I could. Some of us actually have jobs.'

'We have a job, kid.' Red frowned. 'It's our

37

job to investigate weird stuff, remember? Stuff like missing Yeti Chiefs.'

'And a fat lot of help you're being!' Genghis grumped. *'I'm not sure why I bothered coming here. If the wish frog's not going to help, then what's the point? And maybe you're all wrong anyway. Maybe the kidnapper didn't take Bert to trick me into showing him where the wish frog is. Maybe the kidnapper doesn't even know that the wish frog is even still alive? Maybe the ransom note was a way of saying I have no hope at all of rescuing Bert.'*

I nodded. 'He might as well have sent you in search of the Easter Bunny.'

Donny and Red exchanged a knowing glance. 'The Easter Bunny totally exists, kid.' Red shook her head at me. 'Don't be so naive.'

'Whoever's capable of kidnapping a yeti knows what they're doing.' Donny started to pace up and down. 'They must have planned their every move – left nothing to chance. They knew that Genghis knew the secret location of the wish frog. They knew he'd come looking for him to save Bert. There's every chance they followed Genghis here, and every chance that they're biding their time, waiting to make their next move. '

'Kidnapping me,' the wish frog said with a lazy yawn, stretching out his legs. 'That's what we're waiting for now. '

I couldn't believe the wish frog sounded so calm. If I knew someone was out to kidnap me, I'd be super-scared.

'You're right.' Donny nodded at the wish frog. 'We need to keep you safe. The best place for you is here – with our protection. The death worm can be your personal bodyguard.'

Genghis hissed in protest.

'Surely the first thing we should do is assemble the Ministry of Yetis,' the wish frog yawned. 'Don't worry about me – I can handle myself.'

Donny, Red and Genghis all nodded in agreement.

'What's the Ministry of Yetis?' I asked. 'And why do we need to assemble them?'

'Two words for you, kid,' Red grunted. 'Yeti army.'

Hmm, I wasn't sure I liked the idea of a yeti army. But I could see by their faces that the others didn't agree with me. 'So, how do we assembly this yeti army then?' I said, feeling nervous about the answer I was about to hear.

'The Call of the Yeti,' they all said together.

I tried to remember what I'd read about the Call of the Yeti in the book Donny had given me.

'It's a noise one yeti makes to summon another,' Donny explained, as if reading my mind. 'The call gets passed on by every yeti that hears it. That's how the Ministry knows when to meet in an emergency.'

'Like lighting beacons in the darkness, kid,' Red said with a smile. 'It's a warning sign, a signal.'

'But to do this,' the wish frog said, raising a webbed toe into the air and pointing, 'we need to find a yeti to put out the call.'

'Well, I don't have any yeti numbers on speed dial,' I said. 'Although I'm guessing Donny does.'

'Negative.' Donny shrugged. 'Haven't spoken to a yeti in years. They like to keep to themselves, if you know what I mean.'

'Speak for yourself,' Genghis said, sounding annoyed. *'I've been hanging out with yetis for decades.'*

'Me too,' added the frog.

'OK, this isn't a competition,' I said. 'We're in this together, remember.'

'Not many yetis in this part of the world,' the frog said thoughtfully. 'It's too crowded. Yetis are like me. They like the quiet life.'

Donny clapped his hands. 'OK, everyone, it's decided! The first step in the plan is to find a yeti.'

'What then?' I asked.

Donny smiled breezily. 'Simple. Find a yeti, put out the call, assemble the Ministry of Yetis, find Bert and save the wish frog from a terrible fate.'

Simple? Nothing in my life is ever simple! I guess I just need to take a leaf out of the wish frog's book and go with the flow. Nothing seems to bother that little guy. The only problem is that going with the flow always seems to make my life even weirder . . .

Sunday 28th June

Feral Zoo today = hotter than the sun! Seriously, if this heatwave gets any more intense I'm going to march with the penguins to the South Pole and set up home in an igloo.

I AM BOILING!!!!

It's too hot even to think, which is a total bummer. I need all my brain power to figure out how we're going to put out the Call of the Yeti and summon the Ministry of Yetis. But I'm way too unlucky to just have yetis to worry about. Right now I have another mega-beast causing me grief.

My sister!

This morning I've been busy making sure all the animals have plenty of shade and water. As I was seeing to Khan, our grouchy Sumatran tiger, Grace came bounding into the enclosure and accidentally stepped in tiger poo.

'Ergggg!' She made a disgusted, shouty-girly noise and threw her hands into the air. 'That is *it*!' Tears began to stream down her sweaty face. 'I've had enough of this stupid zoo and the stupid animals and the stupid zoo-keepers. No one understands me!'

'Chill out, sis,' I tried to say.

But Grace didn't want to hear. She bent down and tossed tiger poo at me in anger.

What did I do? What any self-respecting little brother would do – I threw poo back at her. It flew through the air and landed right between her eyes.

Bad move.

Grace barged past me, pushing me on to the poo-covered ground. I could hear her sobbing as she fled for the gorilla enclosures. I will never understand girls!

As I wiped the poo from my eyes, a strange thin hand reached towards me.

'Let me help you up,' said a gravelly voice. The hand grabbed on to my arm and hauled me to my feet as if I was as light as a feather. I scrubbed the last of the poo from my vision and

took a good
look at the
stranger
standing
next to me.

It was a
teenage boy. He
was wearing army-
style combat trousers and a
black vest. His clothes hung
off him as though they were
ten sizes too big. His limbs
were as gangly and lean as
a stick insect's, and his
knobbly head sat on his
neck like a lollipop. His
gaunt face was framed
by spiky black hair and
his eyes shone the colour
of violets.

Er, rewind! Since when did people have violet-coloured eyes?

'You're not meant to be in the tiger enclosure,' I said, confused.

He smiled as if I'd said something funny. 'Tigers don't scare me. I'm looking for Donny.'

'SAMMY!' screamed Mum's voice. I turned around to see her marching towards me. 'What have you done to upset your sister?'

'Me?' I yelled back. 'She started it! Why do I always get the blame?'

'Just go and get cleaned up before the sun cakes that poo on to your face for good,' Mum snapped.

I turned back to the boy. 'How do you know . . . ?' But the boy had disappeared.

Am I suffering from heat exhaustion? Or poo-induced madness? Did I imagine him?

I walked out of the tiger enclosure. Past the

Komodo dragons, the Galapagos tortoises and the pygmy hippos and straight to the Backstage gates. When I arrived at the Backstage offices I forgot all about the strange black-haired boy. I forgot to mention him to Donny or anyone else. There's something about the sight of a Mongolian death worm splashing about in a kitchen sink with a wish frog that makes all other thoughts disappear.

'Move over, worm-breath, there's only room for one of us in here, and I'm the last of my kind!' the wish frog croaked as he splashed about in the water.

'*I need to keep my skin moist too, you know!*' Genghis argued back, trying to wedge his fat body further into the sink. '*This heat will bring my sensitive skin out in boils, and three guesses what a death-worm skin-boil is filled with?*'

'Poisonous pus?' I suggested, as I walked over to Donny.

'This zoo isn't big enough for the two of us!' the frog replied grumpily.

'Well, until we've found Bert you two will just have to learn to get along,' Red said. 'If I can get along with poo-face CSC boy here,' she smirked at the tiger poo still smeared on my face, 'then anything's possible.'

Honestly, who needs a sarcastic death worm when you have Red?

'With any luck we'll have Bert back super-soon,' Donny said. 'I've started taking steps to locate him. I've sent the ransom note off to my laboratory to have it analysed for fingerprints and dust particles. With any luck that will give us a clue as to who's taken Bert, and where he's being kept.'

'Good thinking.' I nodded.

'And I have a lead on a nearby yeti.' Donny smiled. 'Let's hope we can persuade her to put out the call.'

'Awesome!' I said. 'What's her name?'

'Jane. She's an old friend of mine from way back. I thought she'd moved back to Nepal, but it turns out she lives just down the road in the woods.'

'What are we waiting for?' I grinned. 'Let's go find her!'

'We're leaving first thing tomorrow, kid,' Red replied. 'Yetis get kind of cranky in the evening. It's best to get them first thing after daylight.'

'But I have school tomorrow!' I pointed out.

'I vote we go nowhere without Sammy,' the wish frog chimed in.

'We can't afford to wait.' Donny looked at me apologetically. 'I've been brushing up on my Yeti. I'm sure we can manage.'

'Both Genghis and I speak Yeti,' the wish frog pointed out. 'That's not the point. The point is that we need to work as a team – the

50

more of us there are, the more hope we have of convincing Jane to help us.'

'I'm sorry.' Donny shook his head. 'We can't afford to lose any time.'

The wish frog looked annoyed and Red just smirked at me.

'That is SO unfair!' I shouted. School is the bane of my life!

Monday 29th June

I'm still melting in the epic heatwave. I hardly slept a wink last night it was so hot. My sheets were soaked through this morning. 'Yuck, Sammy,' Natty wrinkled her nose at me over breakfast this morning. 'You stink like a skunk's armpit.'

'Have you taken a shower?' Mum quizzed.

BUSTED! No time for washing when I'm up all night worrying about kidnapped yetis, endangered wish frogs and dodging death-worm spit!

After a mega-quick shower (which did make me feel much less sticky) I grabbed my lunchbox and left for school. I met Mark, my best friend, at the school gates like I do every day.

A few things about Mark:

* He doesn't know about my ex-werewolf family.

* He doesn't know about Donny and Red's strange job.

* He doesn't know that I can talk to weird animals.

* He tells the worst jokes known to man.

'Hey, Sammy,' Mark said as we walked into class, 'what's a pig's favourite karate move? A pork chop! Get it?'

I didn't even pretend to laugh.

'What's up?' Mark asked as we sat down in class. Mark's known me all my life. He can tell when something's bothering me.

'Don't you ever think that school's a total waste of time?' I asked him.

'Every day.' He grinned like a chimp. 'But if we didn't go to school, what else would we do?'

Err, go off in search of yetis!

'This heat is killing me!' Mark complained as he pulled his books from his bag. 'Mum said if it was any hotter, they'd have to close the school.'

'Really?' I shook my head. No way would I ever get that lucky.

'Yep.' Mark nodded. 'Imagine if something happened to the school water supply. Or if the class windows jammed. We'd all boil to death!'

Saying something like that is typical of Mark's parents. They're the most overprotective worriers I've ever met. They try to make Mark wear gloves every time he holds Beelzebub in case he picks up a weird skin disease.

But maybe they had a point. Maybe if there was some way I could get the school closed down . . . then I'd be free to go yeti hunting.

My phone beeped in my pocket just as Mr Lewis started to write today's maths problem on the board. It was a text from Donny.

> Sammy, u seen the wish frog?
> He's disappeared!

I texted back straight away:

> NO!!!!!!! U think he's
> been kidnapped 2?

This was not good news. Genghis must have led the kidnapper straight to the wish frog, and before we even had a chance to protect him he'd been taken too.

I HAD to get out of school. Now, more than

ever, I needed to be with Donny and the gang. Not only did I not want to miss the yeti hunt, I had to help find the frog!

I took my lunchbox to the dining room and sat down with Mark and Tommy. I ignored their conversation as I tried to think up a plan to bust myself out of school.

'You've been mega-quiet today, Sammy,' Tommy commented as he tucked into his peanut-butter sandwiches. 'Busy thinking up new ways to train a mongoose?'

'No, he's just worried about the black widow spiders eating themselves into extinction,' Mark joked.

If only my friends knew the truth. It would boggle their brains into meltdown! I silently opened up my lunchbox and froze in shock as I peered down at what was inside.

The wish frog leaped from my box straight into the nearest glass of water. He landed

head first, getting
wedged in at his
bum, his hind legs
kicking about
in the air above
him.

'Phew!' he
croaked in Wish
Frog, pulling the
top half of his body
from the glass and
perching on the rim. 'I was
boiling to death in there!'

People around me started to scream their
lungs out and Tommy stood up in shock,
knocking his chair over.

'FROG!!!!!!!' everyone shrieked.

'Nothing to look at here!' I panicked,
picking up the glass of water and rushing to
the nearest exit.

Mark was hot on my heels, cornering me in the school corridor. 'Why are you keeping an Amazon horned frog in your lunchbox? You could have killed it!'

'It's my new pet,' I said, thinking as fast as a cheetah's hind legs. 'I have no idea how it got there.' I looked down at the wish frog angrily.

'I've seen you Ferals eat weird things before,' Mark said anxiously. 'I mean, just the other day I saw Natty eating the zoo otter feed, and I swear I've seen Grace munch on piranha snacks in the aquarium.'

'What can I say?' I laughed nervously. 'Growing up in the zoo has given us strange habits.'

'But live frogs for lunch?' Mark raised an eyebrow.

'I told you, he's a new pet. Except –' I leaned in and whispered – 'my parents don't know about him. The truth is, I stole some frogspawn from the zoo and grew this little guy myself in a jar in my sock draw.'

'Cool!' Mark gasped. 'I can't believe you didn't tell me about him.' He sounded let down.

'Do me a favour and keep it a secret?' I pleaded.

'OK, but you need to tell me what you've been thinking about all day. It annoys me when you go all quiet, Sammy. I start to think you're plotting world snake domination or something weird.'

'Fine.' I sighed, desperate to get Mark off my case. 'The truth is, I'm trying to find a way to get the school closed down.'

Mark's face flushed with horror.

'Not for good,' I reassured him. 'Just for a day or so. It's so hot outside, we shouldn't be cooped up in a classroom.'

Just like frogs shouldn't be cooped up in lunchboxes, the wish frog croaked.

59

Thank goodness he was speaking Wish Frog and not English. How would I ever explain a talking frog to Mark?

'You have a plan?' Mark asked suspiciously.

'Yeah, and I need your help. Meet me by the caretaker's cabin in five minutes.'

I had just enough time to text Donny before I swung my plan into action:

> Found the WF. He was hiding in my lunchbox. Send Red 2 pick him up.

Donny texted back straight away:

> Phew! We've turned the zoo upside down looking. Haven't had a chance 2 visit Jane the yeti. Will go tomorrow. Red's on her way 4 the frog now.

'What were you playing at?' I said angrily to the frog as we headed off towards the caretaker's cabin. 'You could have died in my lunchbox!

And everyone has been so worried about you. You know they have to wait until tomorrow to visit Jane now.'

'That's exactly why I hopped off.' He grinned his wide, froggy mouth at me. 'I knew they wouldn't go without me. And I wanted to find a way to make sure you were there. I hopped to your house and hid in your lunchbox so we could figure out a way to get you out of school. Looks like you didn't need my help though. You've come up with a plan all by yourself!'

I shook my head. 'We need to have serious words with Genghis about his standards of frog-guarding!'

'Actually,' the frog started to explain, 'death worms are very easily distracted. All you have to do is—'

'Shhhh!' I whispered. Mark was standing by the school caretaker's cabin, his back against the wall. He beamed at me as I approached.

'What do you need me to do?' he asked in excitement.

'Distract the caretaker. I need him to leave his cabin for a few minutes.'

Mark gave me the playful grin that I knew so well. 'Done. Hey, Sammy,' he smirked, 'what's a frog's favourite drink? Croak-a-cola!' The wish frog let out a groan and I forced a smile.

'Help! Help! Help!' Mark started to scream at the top of his lungs. 'Help!'

The school caretaker rushed from his cabin and slammed straight into Mark. 'What's wrong, lad?'

'I just saw one of the older kids throw a rock through a science-block window. I think they've gone on a rampage!'

'Those little tykes!' the caretaker swore. And with that he ran off towards to the science blocks. I only had a few minutes before he'd come back.

I looked around desperately for Red – I needed her! Then I saw her bright red hair in the distance. 'Red!'

She ran over. 'Where's the frog, kid?'

'I need your help with something, quickly!'

I hurriedly slipped into the hut without anyone seeing me, the wish frog still perched on the edge of the water glass in my hand. Red followed me, confused.

'We don't have much time. But you need to trust me and help with something.'

'OK,' she said seriously.

Sure, Red can be nastier than a scorpion with anger issues, but she's great in a crisis. And I can trust her with anything.

'What do you need me to do?' she asked.

'See that pipe over there?' I pointed up to the school's main water supply, which ran through the caretaker's cabin. 'I need you to put it out of action for me.'

Red flashed me a mischievous grin. 'Consider it done.'

She stared at the pipe. Red does that when she's using her powers of telekinesis; she has to concentrate really hard to move things with her thoughts. Her eyes squinted in concentration as her mind bent the metal pipe as if it was a plastic drinking straw. The pipe groaned and creaked, and before long water started spurting out of it.

The wish frog hopped out of the glass of water and into the puddles collecting on the cabin floor.

'Hey, get back in . . .' But my words were drowned out by the sound of the water pipe splitting in two and a waterfall crashing down on to the floor.

'Woo hoo!' croaked the wish frog in delight. 'I haven't had this much fun since I surfed down the Amazon on the back of a flying fish!'

I bent down, trying to catch him as he slipped from my hands. He hopped about, splashing in the puddles and riding the crashing waves as if they were a roller coaster. 'Yahoo!!!!!!'

In the distance I could hear Mark's voice. 'I'm so sorry, I could have sworn I saw a smashed window. It's this heat – it's playing tricks on my brain.'

'We need to get out of here,' I said in desperation. 'If we're caught, they'll know it was us who busted the school water supply!'

Red stared at the wish frog, who was too busy having fun to listen to a word I said. She summoned him into her hands with the power of her mind.

'Hey!' he protested.

We ran from the hut just in time to escape unnoticed. I was soaked right through – and I was going to have mega-trouble trying to explain why.

'I'll take him back to the zoo,' Red said, gesturing to the seriously annoyed wish frog. 'See you tomorrow for yeti hunting?'

'I'll be there at sunrise,' I assured her.

As you can imagine, the rest of the day was chaos.

Word soon got round that the main water pipe had burst, and before long every kid in school was dancing in the waterfall that gushed into the playground.

With no water, and a heatwave to rival the Sahara Desert, school was closed down within the hour.

'School will be suspended until further notice!' the headmaster announced as everyone ran from the school gate in glee.

'Nice work, Sammy.' Mark slapped my hand with a high five as we walked away from the chaos. 'That was epic! And now we've got tomorrow off school. I'll come to the zoo and hang out.'

'Sure,' I smiled. 'I'm gonna sleep late though, so come by after lunch.'

With any luck, I'll be back at the zoo by then, with Jane the yeti safely Backstage and ready to summon the Ministry of Yetis. Then Mark and I can kick back in the bug house and watch tarantulas hatch until it's time to be dragged back to school.

Today = total success.

I.AM.A.LEGEND!

Tuesday 30th June

I was at the zoo before sunrise. And at this time of year, sunrise is pretty early in the morning so I'm mega-tired right now. I've got a lot to write down, it's been a busy day, so I'll try to keep this as snappy as a crocodile at a fish farm.

Last night I warned Mum and Dad not to expect me at breakfast. I told them that I was making the most of having the day off school by getting to the zoo in time to catch the flying squirrels in action. Everyone knows that the best time to check out nocturnal mammals is before dawn.

The woods where Jane the yeti lives are only an hour away. Donny drove his van through the darkness. Red sat in the front and I sat in the back between Genghis and the wish frog. Just sitting between a death

worm and a wish frog in a van is a healthy level 4 on the Feral Scale of Weirdness, I'd say.

'This is not what I signed up for when I came to Feral Zoo,' yawned the wish frog. 'I just wanted to relax in my bug tank and ride the retirement wave all the way to the sleepy shore.'

'I've just remembered something,' I blurted out. Donny's eyes met mine in the driver's mirror. 'I forgot to tell you about this really weird boy I met in the zoo the other day.'

'Weird how?' Donny asked, curious.

'I don't know.' I shrugged, suddenly feeling stupid for mentioning it. 'He was in the tiger enclosure, said he was looking for you.'

'What did he look like?' Red frowned.

'Mega-lanky. Black hair,' I described. 'Maybe it was the fact I was looking at him through a film of tiger poo, but I swear his eyes were a funny shade of purple.'

The tyres of Donny's van screeched on the tarmac and we swerved to the side of the road. The force of the stop made me swing around, so I was face to face with Genghis. I let out an almighty howl and scrunched my eyes shut in panic.

Death by worm stare is no way to go!

'Ant!' Donny shouted.

'My name's Sammy and you nearly killed me!' I shouted back.

'Ant – he's a kid with purple eyes and black hair. We used to be colleagues . . . friends even. I haven't seen him for years. If he's lurking around the zoo, then we most definitely have problems.'

'If anyone's strong enough to kidnap a yeti, then it's Ant,' Red said with worry in her voice. 'We should have known.'

Whoa – rewind! What kind of teenager is strong enough to overpower a yeti? Anyway, Ant looks like a giant weed!

'Explain, please,' I urged Donny.

'Explain and drive,' said Red, annoyed.

Donny restarted the engine, took a deep breath and told me all about Ant.

ANT

Age: 16

Ability: Like an ant, he can lift more than 20 times his own body weight!

Looks like: Body of a spindly ant with violet insect-like eyes

Can be found: Plotting ways to become the most powerful creature alive

'Never judge a book by its cover,' the wish frog said. 'And never judge a tiny ant to have less power than a mighty lion.'

'I've told you before, Sammy,' Donny said as I scratched my head in confusion, 'I collect weirdos – people with strange powers and abilities. Ant was one of the first weirdos I ever met.' Donny parked the van in dense woodland. We all got out and began to walk through the trees. 'Just like an ant, he's freakishly strong, and just like an ant, he's willing to fight to the death. He might look harmless and weedy, but he's deadly!'

A boy like an ant? I was seriously baffled.

'OK, so we know that Ant would be strong enough to overpower a yeti, but I don't get what he'd want with the wish frog?'

Donny sighed. 'Ant used to be one of the good guys. He'd help me solve crypto-cases. But soon that wasn't enough. He wanted more. I guess it's hard dealing with weird powers.'

'Sammy and I seem to cope,' Red said bitterly.

Hmm, if you ask me, Red's just one bad-hair day away from becoming a super-villain. She definitely has serious baddy potential.

'Ant is obsessed with power. Like a queen commanding a colony of worker ants, he wants the whole world to bow down to him.' Donny led us deeper into the woods. It was beginning to get light, but I could still hear the tooting of night owls and rustling of badgers and hedge-hogs in the mossy ground. 'He'll do anything to make that happen.'

'Even kidnap a yeti?' Genghis asked sceptically.

'We don't even know for sure that it is Ant we're dealing with,' I said carefully. I'd only seen the boy once and I didn't want us resting every hope we had on it definitely being him.

Before I knew it, we arrived at what looked like a huge boulder. A boulder as big as a house. In front of the boulder was a fallen tree, hollow and moss-covered.

Donny kicked away some mouldy leaves from the bottom of the tree to reveal what looked like a badger hole. 'I can't believe she still lives here, after all these years,' he muttered.

Donny scrambled, face first, down into the hole. Red followed him without question and Genghis wriggled in behind. 'After you,' the wish frog croaked at me.

When did jumping into a muddy hole lead to anything but trouble?

'Oh no,' I said politely. 'You first.'

The frog narrowed his bulging eyes. 'A journey of a thousand miles must start with a single step.' And with that, he leaped into the hole.

I got down on my knees and peered into the hole's blackness. I stuck my head in. It smelt like damp leaves and fox wee.

And then I fell. I fell for ages . . . and ages . . .

I hit the ground – hard! I rubbed at where my head had bashed against the ground as my eyes adjusted to a gloomy cave.

The cave stank of rotten cabbage and stale farts. Totally puke-inducing! In the corner was what looked like a woolly mammoth. It was the colour of sand, hunched over like a gorilla. The monster threw its arms wide and let out a growl that could deafen an elephant.

'Nooooooo!' the beast shouted. 'What are you doing here? I just want to be left alone!'

Donny was standing facing the beast. His arms were folded across his chest and he looked annoyed. If there's anyone in the world who wouldn't flinch as a yeti screamed at them, it's Donny.

I tiptoed towards them. My heart was pounding my ribs like a mighty gorilla beating its chest. I'd never seen a yeti before – I'd never really given much thought to what they looked like. But the picture I had in my head was nothing like the creature that stood in front of me. This thing was terrifying!

Jane stood up and her head skimmed the cave's ceiling. She was gargantuan – nearly three metres tall and as broad as two mighty silverbacks. As I crept closer, I could see her face. She had a muzzle like an ape, huge bristly eyebrows and teeth as yellow and sharp as rusty daggers.

'What are you

doing in my home?' The yeti's voice simmered with rage and the air crackled with the power behind it.

A strange sound came from Donny's lips. *'A feesy piddle wobble blurg,'* he said.

'What are you doing?' I whispered.

'Speaking Yeti,' he replied.

'No, you're not,' I said. I stepped nervously forward and looked the yeti in the eye. *'This is my colleague Donny,'* I said in Yeti.

Jane nodded in recognition. *'I've met Donny before. But who are you?'*

'I'm Sammy Feral,' I told her. *'And this is Red.'* Red was shuffling nervously. I'd never seen her look scared before.

'Genghis, I haven't seen you for years,' Jane muttered at him.

'This is the wish frog.' I pointed at the small frog on the floor.

Jane turned and looked at me with thunder

in her eyes. I felt my knees knock and my feet quiver in my trainers.

For the record, looking a yeti in the eye $=$ pure terror.

'*We're here because we need your help,*' I stammered. Jane's eyes lit up like coals, and just when I thought she was going to take my head off with one swipe of her giant paws, she nodded for me to continue.

I told her everything. I told her about Bert being kidnapped, and Genghis coming to us for help. I told her about the wish frog living at the zoo for years. And I told her about Ant coming to the zoo. The others looked on in amazement as I chatted away in Yeti as if it was my mother tongue.

'*We don't know for sure that Ant is behind the kidnapping,*' I added nervously.

'*So . . .*' Jane said thoughtfully. She sat on the cave floor and I felt the earth tremble slightly as she plonked herself down. '*Bert finally got what was coming to him.*'

'*Look, I know you two had your differences in recent years,*' Genghis said gently.

'*Differences?*' Jane spat as she spoke. '*He broke my heart! We were meant to be together, just me and him. Live in a cave and bring yeti cubs into the world. He abandoned me!*'

'*Oh, cry me a river! He had a duty,*' Genghis argued in perfect Yeti. '*He was voted Yeti Chief. And he deserved it too. Think of all the people he's helped! All the lives he's saved along the way!*'

'*Well, I hope Ant breaks every bone in his body,*' Jane growled as tears gathered in her giant eyes.

'*You don't mean that,*' I said quietly. '*My sisters do mean things to me all the time, but I wouldn't wish harm on them. I'd do anything to protect them – I'm sure you feel the same way about Bert.*'

81

Jane started wailing and crying. Yeti snot started streaming from her huge nostrils – gushing like the waterfall from the burst pipe at school yesterday.

'*You're right!*' she howled. '*I'll always love him! He's the most courageous, kind and thoughtful yeti I know. I can't bear to think of him in pain. I have to help! I'll put out the call and summon a yeti army that could defeat the deadliest of enemies!*'

SUCCESS!

I punched the air in triumph!

'*Take me back to your base,*' Jane said, standing up and nearly knocking her head on the cave roof. '*I'm ready to fight!*'

Jane didn't have anything to pack. She lifted us up, one by one, so we could climb out of the cave and back into the woods. Then she followed us back through the trees to Donny's van.

'We can put out the call as soon as we get back,' I said as we sped back to the zoo.

'*Sammy,*' Jane whispered in a growl. We were crammed into the van like elephants trying to walk through an ant tunnel. '*I'm worried I've been living alone too long. My voice isn't as strong as it used to be.*'

'*But you can still make a yeti call?*' Genghis asked anxiously.

'*Oh, I can make the call all right,*' Jane said as Donny revved the engine, '*but I'm not sure it will be loud enough. And there's another problem too.*'

'*What?*' I asked quickly.

'*The Call of the Yeti takes weeks to summon yetis from all over the world,*' Jane explained. '*If we put out the call tonight, if we're lucky it will reach the ears of one, maybe two other yetis. But then they must summon their nearest neighbours, and they in turn must summon those closest to them. It'll take weeks before every yeti in the world arrives at the zoo.*'

That was a problem. Time was not on our side and we couldn't afford to wait weeks. I quickly translated what Jane had said to everyone else.

'This isn't good. We need to assemble the Ministry of Yetis quickly,' Donny said, concerned.

'I have an idea,' said the wish frog. 'But it'll take a miracle to pull off.'

'Well, I don't know about miracles,' I said, 'but we do have a cryptozoologist, Red's telekinesis, a yeti, a death worm and the wish frog on our side.'

'We've had enough drama for one day,' the frog said wearily. 'Let's go home. Eat, sleep and meet at the zoo first thing tomorrow. And get ready to break the law . . .'

Today was a cranked-up eight on the Feral Scale of Weirdness. I still don't know what the wish frog's plan is. But I do know one thing: I totally blanked out and forgot to meet Mark at the zoo after lunch. He had to spend the afternoon picking up porcupine needles with Max. And tonight I had some terrible news – the school water pipe is fixed so I have to go back to school tomorrow.

I texted Donny as I was falling asleep:

Have to go to skol tomoz. I'll be Backstage 4 meeting as quickly as I can. The WF won't do anything without me – you'll have to wait!

Wednesday 1st July

What is moodier than a pygmy hippo with a height complex, stinks of perfume and has to pluck her nostril hair once a week?

My big sister!

Grace's argument with Max this afternoon was so explosive it could have melted polar ice caps!

I was hurrying past the birds of prey, towards Backstage, when I heard Grace yelling. I couldn't even decipher what she was saying — only other ex-werewolves with super-dog hearing could understand such a squeal. She stormed towards me, shouting wildly — anyone would think she'd just been attacked by a flock of rabid turkey vultures! 'NEVER SPEAK TO THAT TRAITOR MAX AGAIN!!!'

Er, OK, Grace. Actually I think I can decide who I can and cannot speak to.

'You have to help me, Sammy,' Max pleaded, as I tried to run past him.

'I'm not getting involved.' I tried to wriggle free from his grasp.

'I'm moving away,' Max said sadly. 'Grace and I will be apart, but I can't live without her! She's my moon, my stars, my every . . .'

Excuse me while I throw up!

'OK, hold it, Romeo.' I scrunched my eyes shut and held up my hands. 'I'll puke all over your shoes if you say any more!'

'I've been given a place at a zoology college on the other side of the country.' He sighed and his shoulders slumped. 'I want to go to the Royal College of Zoology – it's much nearer. But I don't have the experience to get in.'

Max is one of the best zookeepers around – the Royal College of Zoology would be lucky to have him.

'You've been working here for years,' I pointed out. 'You know more about the life cycle of reptiles than anyone I know.'

'The college wants me to write a project on rehabilitating a rare animal. I suggested the okapi, but someone got there first.'

'Leave it with me,' I said, my mind spinning with ideas. There were enough rare animals

Backstage to fill a library. 'I'll find you something to write about.'

'And no werewolves,' Max whispered. 'The longer we can keep werewolves a secret the better.'

'Agreed.'

Geez! As if I didn't have enough to worry about. Now I have to help Romeo and Juliet. I should change my name to Sammy Superman Feral and be done with it!

Donny, Red and the animal freak brigade were waiting for me Backstage.

'Where've you been all day?' Jane asked. I looked up at her giant body looming over me and gulped. I'd almost forgotten how terrifying she looked – and smelt!

Not only does she look like Bigfoot, but she smells like Bigfoot's athlete's foot and has teeth like rotten toenails!

I inched backwards as Jane stomped nearer

to me. *'I need you to translate for me. Listening to Donny try to speak Yeti is painful,'* she said.

Donny was sat on an upturned crate, hunched over a Yeti dictionary. He scowled as he flicked through the pages and uttered sounds that sounded nothing like Yeti.

Red stormed out of the Backstage offices, her bright red hair flying out behind her. Genghis writhed at her feet and the wish frog hopped lazily behind her. 'If we had to wait any longer, kid, my hair would have been as grey as Donny's. The frog wouldn't tell us anything about his "master plan" until you arrived. Well, he's here now, frog face.' She turned and glared at the wish frog. 'So get croaking!'

The wish frog hopped lazily on to the crate that Donny sat on. 'Gather round.'

Donny got up and we all huddled around the crate so we could hear the frog speak.

'Has anyone heard of the BBC World Service

radio station?' the frog said, with the smallest hint of a smile.

'Sure,' Red said curiously. 'But what do you know about radio? You're a frog.'

The frog let out an irritated grunt. 'What don't I know about radio? I've granted wishes for every music megastar of the last century: the Beatles, Britney, Beyoncé, Bieber . . . Did I ever tell you about the time I was on a tour bus with Madonna and—'

'*Oh, please, tell us one of your pointless stories while Bert is being tortured to death,*' spat Genghis, his acidic saliva sizzling on the ground.

'Hey, chillax.' The frog raised his webbed foot in protest. 'Experience is education for the soul. I could teach you a thing or two about—'

'He's sorry,' I apologized quickly as Genghis grumbled something about attention seeking. 'You were saying?'

The frog blinked lazily. 'I was saying that we need to break into the BBC World Service. There we'll find radio transmitters powerful enough to reach every corner of the globe.'

I quickly translated for Jane. Her eyes lit up with excitement. '*We could contact every yeti on earth in a matter of seconds.*'

'I've got to give it to you, Wish Frog –' Donny beamed – 'that is genius.'

'He's right,' Red agreed. 'A traditional yeti call would take weeks. But this will summon the Ministry of Yetis in days – maybe hours if we're lucky.'

'It's hardly a perfect plan,' Genghis said grudgingly, *'but it will have to do.'*

'We need to break into the radio station first,' I pointed out. 'And that'll take planning.'

'We leave tomorrow night,' Donny said thoughtfully. 'That'll give us enough time to prepare for the mission.'

'Any news on those lab results?' I asked Donny. 'Did you find any fingerprints on the ransom note?'

'Nothing.' Donny shook his head. 'We'll need to find another way to track Ant and Bert down. But let's get through tomorrow first.'

When I think about tomorrow, my heart

beats faster than the hoofs of a galloping racehorse.

This isn't the first time I've broken into a building. Donny and Red once helped me break into my school and steal mercury from the science labs. But that was different — the fate of my family was at stake!

This time I'm breaking the law for someone I don't even know.

But if everyone else is prepared to risk their life for Bert, then he must be mega-important. I can't back out now. We're a team.

Until tomorrow, goodnight . . .

Thursday 2nd July

Right now I'm more nervous than the time we had to wait three weeks before the zoology council announced that the Yoda bat was real.

School is nearly over for the day. I'm writing this under my desk in French class. Concentrating in French is hard enough, but on top of that Mark just whispered in my ear, 'The fact is, you're not very reliable, Sammy.'

That sucks. I hate that he thinks that about me.

'But for all your flaws, you pulled off the most epic school prank in history the other day.'

'Prank?' I whispered back.

'Yeah, the water pipe – getting the school closed down. That one's going in the history books for sure.'

Madame Lark gave us the evil eye and we froze silently. As soon as her back was turned, Mark whispered again, 'But I need to know I can rely on you when the time comes.'

'I'm really reliable when it matters.'

'Cos I'm planning the school prank to end all others – and I want you to be a part of it. Can I trust you?'

No way do I want Mark to think I'm a bad friend, but I also don't want to agree to something I can't deliver. 'What's the prank?' I asked.

He shrugged. 'We need to think of one.'

The only thing I can think of right now is tonight.

7 P.M.

I ran to the zoo first thing after school. My palms were sweating and my head was racing. Not long to go until the BBC break-in!

Max cornered me by the rhinos. 'About that rare animal you were going to hook me up with?'

Talk about bad timing! I tried to edge past him. 'Now's not a good time.'

He stood in front of me and folded his arms. 'You're the one who has to live with Grace – the longer you leave it, the worse she'll get.'

He had a point.

'OK, come Backstage. But you have to swear that you won't breathe a word of this to another living soul.'

Max crossed his heart. I led him Backstage.

I must be suffering from serious brain-melt right now, because what I did next was stupider than a beaver in a beret.

Before I knew it we were standing in front of the Mongolian death worm. 'Whatever you do, don't look it in the eye.'

'Is it some kind of giant snake?' Max reached to stroke him and Genghis let out an almighty hiss. Spit flew from his fangs and Max leaped back in horror. 'What *is* that?'

'That,' I tried to sound cool, 'is a Mongolian death worm.'

Max looked at me as though I'd just spoken to him in Martian. 'It's a poisonous worm that can kill you with a single stare. Oh, and it can understand English but can't speak it. Maybe you could give it lessons as part of your rehabilitation project.'

Max looked at me with horror. 'I asked if you could help me rehabilitate a rare animal. Not teach a Mongolian death worm to speak!'

Sometimes I wonder why I bother.

'It's the best I could do on such short notice,'

I snapped at Max. 'I'm sure he'll make an excellent case study. Just write up your notes and then exchange the words 'worm' for 'snake', and 'speak' for 'eat' – you'll write a masterpiece!'

Max did not look convinced.

'Er, did I miss the part where I agreed to this?' Genghis objected. *'I will not be studied like a freak of nature!'*

'You are a freak of nature,' I said. 'And you're currently living here at the zoo for free. You can consider this your rent payment.'

He wrinkled his wormy skin in disgust. *'Ugh, life is like a roller coaster and I'm about to throw up!'*

'So, I'll, umm, see you back here tomorrow?' Max said nervously. 'I'll bring my laptop and some English books.'

'And some protective eyewear,' I advised.

Max walked off, looking thoroughly confused. I don't blame him – it's not every day you discover there's such a thing as Mongolian death worms.

If this afternoon was a healthy six on the Feral Scale of Weirdness, then tonight is going to shatter records. We're on our way to the BBC World Service station right now. I snuck out of my bedroom window and climbed down the drainpipe. Mum would KILL me if she knew!

We're driving in Donny's van. I'm in the back again and Jane is crammed into the boot. I can hear her growling. I feel sick. Will write again once this is over . . .

11.30 P.M.

The BBC World Service radio station is in central London. Even in the middle of the night, the streets were brightly lit and cars whizzed by at top speed. There was more chance of a yeti becoming the next president of the USA than of us sneaking into the BBC unnoticed.

Donny parked his van outside the radio station and spread out a blueprint of the building on his lap. He shone a torch on to the map. 'We take this entrance here.' He pointed to a side door. 'Then we climb up through this air vent and scramble . . .'

'I'm not sure I'll fit in an air vent,' Jane said, as if she could read my mind.

'Less yeti talk, more action,' Red said sternly. She threw a blanket at Jane. 'Put this over your head, and carry Genghis.'

'I can wriggle myself,' Genghis protested.

Jane picked him up, cradled him in her

smelly armpit and threw the blanket over them both. It was the worst disguise I'd ever seen. The blanket only covered her head and shoulders. You could still see her hairy body and her Bigfoot legs – not to mention the fact that she was nearly three metres tall and carrying a giant worm!

'I'm coming with you.' The wish frog jumped into my pocket. 'Don't squish me!'

I shook my head. 'This is never going to work.'

'We need to focus!' Donny said sternly, his hand on the door. 'After me. One . . . two . . .'

He opened the door and sprang out on to the busy London road. Red clambered out and Jane and I followed close behind.

Donny led us down a dark alleyway. A fox sniffing through a rubbish bin looked up and whimpered at the sight of Jane stomping towards him. The fox scampered off and we arrived at a small doorway with a sign that read 'Stage Door'.

Red took one hard look at the door handle and it clicked open. Donny silently stepped inside. He pointed his torch up at the ceiling of a long, dark corridor. There was an air vent right above us. Jane reached up and popped the vent cover off. She silently lifted Donny up and placed him inside the vent, followed by Red.

Then she looked down at me, worry flashing in her yeti eyes. *'I'm not going to fit in there,'* she said simply.

She was right – the air vent looked tiny enough for me to crawl through. But a yeti? No way!

'It's the only way,' Donny whispered from inside the vent. He quickly glanced down at the map of the building he was still holding. 'We need to get up to the signalling tower on the sixth floor. It's too risky to climb the stairs.'

'Donny, we don't have a choice,' I whispered. 'Jane won't fit in there.'

Genghis stuck his head out of Jane's armpit and gasped for breath. *'Your armpit is more toxic than my spit!'*

'Jane – we'll take the stairs,' I said, sounding braver than I felt. The thought of separating from Donny and Red made my knees knock but there was no choice.

'*Really?*' Her eyebrows rose in hope.

I swallowed hard. '*Up to the sixth floor? Sure. How hard can it be?*'

'I'll see you there,' whispered Donny. He and Red scrambled off into the distance.

There was a staircase at the end of the dark corridor. '*Follow me.*' Jane was close behind. She must have been mega-scared – she was sweating way more than usual. It took everything I had not to pass out from the stench.

My heart hammered as we came closer to the stairwell. We passed doors to studios, offices and cupboards. I could hear voices laughing and joking. I scrunched my eyes as I walked and hoped that no one would smell us coming.

A door to my right flung open. '*Back against the wall!*' I hissed in Yeti.

I heard Jane's sharp intake of breath as we pressed ourselves against the corridor wall. A man came out into the corridor and walked the other way without looking back.

PHEW!!!

There was no time to hang about!

'Quickly!' I ran the rest of the length of the corridor, and Jane thumped along the floor behind me. Next thing we were in the stairwell and running up the stairs.

One flight, two flights, three flights . . . 'Not so fast!' complained the wish frog in my jacket pocket. 'I'm getting motion sickness!' Four flights . . . five . . . six.

I threw the stairwell door open at the sixth floor.

Donny stuck his grey head of hair out from behind a door. 'Psst, in here!'

I tiptoed into the small signalling room and Jane squeezed in behind me. *'There's less room in here than there was in the air vent,'* she complained.

Red was staring at a
large radio control
deck. She was
using her mind
to activate the
giant radio
transmitter.
Switches flipped
about and lights
flickered to life.

'We're ready to go,' she told us. 'We'll be going live to all continents, both poles and across every ocean in five, four, three, two . . .'

The wish frog hopped out of my pocket and on to the radio control deck. He placed one frog leg on the 'LIVE ON AIR' switch and looked at Jane. *'Give it your best shot. We can only do this once . . .'*

The switch flicked to ON and a green light started to flash. I held my breath as Jane bent down and leaned into the microphone. She closed her eyes and her eyelids twitched in concentration. Her lips quivered as she opened her mouth.

Then came the sound . . .

Donny and Red clamped their hands over their ears and Genghis's body scrunched up in shock. The wish frog leaped back into my pocket and I felt the skin on my face ripple like a wave.

The walls of the small room began to shake and the ground beneath me trembled like in an earthquake.

CRACK!

SMASH!

The windows shattered into thousands of tiny shards of glass around me.

The Call of the Yeti = most ear-shattering noise EVER!

But to me it wasn't just a sound. I heard words too.

'Yetis of earth, rise up. Hear my call. I summon you. We must come together. We fight to the death . . .'

What felt like pride swelled within me, and if I had been a yeti, I would have stomped across every country in the world to fight at Jane's side. *'Come to find me . . . find Sammy Feral.'*

'We need to get out of here!' Red shouted. 'Someone's coming!'

'Did it work?' I said, panicking.

Donny looked around for a way out. 'We'll find out soon enough.'

I could hear footsteps running along the hall. If we didn't move soon, I'd be spending my next birthday in jail! There was no time for air vents or stairwells.

'The fire escape!' the wish frog croaked.

The door burst open and a security guard stood in the doorway. He opened his mouth to scream at us and then froze in fear at the sight of Jane.

Jane's big feet pounded the floor as she pushed her way past the guard and down the corridor. We followed her at lightning speed. The fire escape was at the end of the corridor.

Red shattered the door with her mind

and sprinted out on to the fire escape. We all followed her down the creaking metal stairs and were soon back in the dark London alleyway.

I don't think I stopped to take a breath until we had bundled into the van and sped away into the night.

Donny drove us back to the zoo in silence. I was too terrified to speak. We'd destroyed the BBC signalling tower, and probably scared a security guard to death. I just hope the Call of the Yeti worked.

As I write this, every member of the Ministry of Yetis should be making their way to Feral Zoo. I hope I wake up tomorrow and they're all here, ready to fight to the death and bring Bert back.

Now we need to concentrate on finding where Ant is keeping Bert hostage. Once we know where he is, and the yeti army arrives, then we can attack!

Friday 3rd July

School was slower than a tortoise towing an elephant.

Mark won't shut up about the 'Ultimate School Prank'. As if I care!

I didn't hear from Donny all day and I was desperate to get to the zoo to see if any yetis had turned up yet.

'No sign of anyone yet,' Jane grumbled as I ran into the Backstage yard. *'Maybe the call didn't work.'*

My heart sank like the *Titanic*.

'Any luck tracking down Ant yet? So we know where to go once the Ministry does arrive.'

Jane shook her head. *'Nothing new to report. Donny and Red have spread the word on the crypto-scene that we're looking for him.'*

Well, that's something, I guess.

'Your friend's been here all day.' Jane nodded towards Max, who was busy studying Genghis. He'd borrowed a beekeeper's suit from the zoo bug house. He looked like an astronaut!

I plodded towards him with a heavy heart.

'I thought protection was key to the success of this project,' Max mumbled through his thick white suit. 'Better safe than sorry. I'm teaching it nursery rhymes.'

'It?' Genghis said, spitting manically on purpose. He then launched into the most acid spit-tastic rendition of 'Twinkle, Twinkle, Little Star' I've ever heard. Honestly, I thought the Call of the Yeti was bad. But the sound of a death worm serenading me was enough to make me deaf for life!

'Excellent work!' I commended Max.

Worst thing about today = no yetis.

Best thing = seeing a Mongolian death worm learning English!

Saturday 4th July

I woke up this morning to the sound of Mum screaming.

Soon I could hear Grace shrieking, Natty wailing and Dad making a spluttering sound like a fish out of water. And poor Caliban was howling away as if the moon was full!

I sped down the stairs. 'What is going on?'

There was a yeti standing in my living room. He was stooped over, hunching his back. *'This room is very small,'* he said, scowling. There was a thud behind me and I looked back to see Mum lying unconscious on the floor. Grace rushed to

her side and began fanning her. 'Mum's fainted!'
Natty cried.

'Are you Sammy Feral?' the yeti asked in a deep,
booming voice.

'It's the smell,' Grace said angrily as Mum
came to. 'That stench is enough to floor anyone.

Honestly!' Grace threw her hands into the air. 'Is a normal life too much to ask for?'

'I'm Sammy,' I replied to the yeti. Caliban sniffed at the yeti's big feet and whimpered in confusion. 'You were meant to go to the zoo, not come here.'

'The call said to find Sammy Feral,' the yeti apologized. 'I'm Bob – nice to meet you.' Bob nearly crushed my hand as he shook it enthusiastically.

I introduced the others. 'This is my dad.' Bob shook Dad's hand and Dad clenched his teeth in pain. 'And this is Mum, Grace, Natty and Caliban. We need to get you to the . . .'

The doorbell rang loudly.

'That will be Sid,' Bob said. 'He's travelled all the way from California with his wife and three young cubs.'

Bob wasn't lying. It wasn't even 8 a.m. and I had Bob, Sid and Sid's yeti family squeezed into my living room.

'I'll put the kettle on,' Mum said, looking pale and breathing deeply. 'We'll talk about this later, Sammy,' she growled quietly. Great, now I'm in for a total blasting.

The doorbell went again.

'Sammy!' Mum screamed angrily.

Before we'd even had breakfast we had a total of ten yetis in our house. That's ten times normal yeti stink.

Donny arrived in his van looking delighted. 'The Call of the Yeti worked!'

We crammed as many of the yetis as we could into the van and shuttled them to the zoo. Then Donny went back to collect the others from my house while I showed Bob around Backstage.

'You can all stay here!' I announced proudly, sweeping my arms around at the empty cages and battered-up dens.

'It'll need some work,' Bob grumbled. *'There's*

not many yetis I'd stay in such cramped conditions for, but Bert is special.'

'We'll have to wait a while before the whole Ministry arrives,' Sid said to Bob. *'We can use that time to do some renovation work.'*

But there was no time to sit about and watch the yetis 'renovate' Backstage. Another 30 yetis turned up at my house today. Not long now before the whole Ministry is assembled, surely . . .

'Consider yourself grounded until your 18th birthday!' Mum said crossly this evening. 'The Feral family home is not a yeti holiday destination. And you are NOT to get involved with anything dangerous.'

'Chill out, Mum,' I argued. She would FLIP if she knew what I'd got myself into. Kidnapped Yeti Chiefs, Mongolian death worms and boys with super-strength are not going to sit well with her. 'Donny's just having a few friends visit,' I lied. 'They must have just got lost on the way to the zoo.'

Feral family home turning into a yeti hideout = level 7 on the Feral Scale of Weirdness!

Sunday 5th July

If there's one thing more painful than a jabbing from an angry porcupine, it's the sight of a Mongolian death worm trying to learn English.

'Baa, baa, black sheep . . . Spit. Spit. Spit. Spit. Have you any . . .'

'I told you, worm,' Max shouted angrily. 'Eyes to the ground and easy on the spit! Remember your posture – the more you slouch, the more you spray.'

There were burn marks in the hard tarmac where Genghis's acidic spit had frazzled everything it touched. Max was wearing his beekeeper's suit and he looked stupider than a squirrel riding a motorbike.

Max pulled his heavy mask off. His face was dripping with sweat, but there was a broad smile stretching from ear to ear. 'Mongolian death worms are fascinating creatures, Sammy,' he beamed. 'I've started to write up my report.' He handed me a notebook peppered with acid-burn holes.

I opened Max's project workbook and read what he'd written aloud:

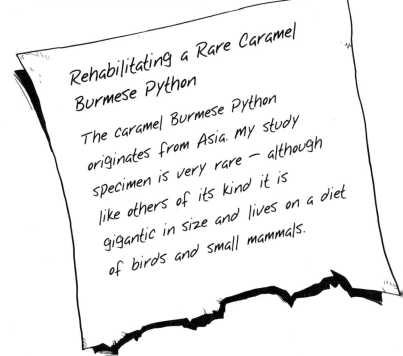

Rehabilitating a Rare Caramel Burmese Python

The caramel Burmese Python originates from Asia. My study specimen is very rare — although like others of its kind it is gigantic in size and lives on a diet of birds and small mammals.

'*I eat large mammals too.*' Genghis grinned, licking his lips at Max.

'Er, this is great,' I told Max, relieved that he couldn't understand Death Worm. 'But Burmese pythons are nearly always found near water,' I pointed out, 'and Mongolian death worms like to live in deserts.'

Max snatched the notebook back. 'If you're just going to pick more holes in my project than a death worm can erode with its spit, then I suggest you keep your nose out of it!'

Jeez! I was only trying to help!

'I've actually come Backstage to see how the yetis are settling in,' I explained.

Max scratched his head. 'Death worms, yetis . . . this place is so weird even the cockroaches will be moving out soon.'

'Sammy!' Donny ran over. His grey hair was sticking up all over the place and he looked seriously stressed. 'You need to go home, NOW!'

'Er, why?'

'Your dad just called – there are more yetis at your house. I'll be over to pick them up as soon as possible. Can you just keep them entertained? For now?'

'You didn't say anything to my dad about Bert being kidnapped, and raising an army of yetis to help find him, did you?' I asked, suddenly panicked.

Donny looked confused. 'No, I didn't mention anything. Did you want me to?'

'NO!' I shouted. 'The less they know about all this dangerous stuff the better.'

Honestly, it's a miracle the neighbours haven't asked questions. I noticed a few twitching curtains this evening, but this wouldn't be the first time we've had a wild animal delivered to the house instead of the zoo by mistake.

Although usually the animals are in cages and driven by zookeepers – they don't just turn up carrying suitcases and whistling yeti songs.

I've put a sign on the door that says:

YETI Fancy Dress Party Here!

PLEASE USE BACK DOOR!

Words cannot describe the level of puke-inducing toxic fumes that have invaded my house since the first yeti turned up. Honestly, I'd rather hang out in a den of skunks after they'd run a marathon! Grace is walking around with a perfumed hankie tied around her head, and Natty keeps making dramatic retching noises. This Ministry of Yetis needs to get to work FAST! Otherwise my house will turn into one giant stink bomb!

'Let's hold this Ministry meeting tomorrow,' I urged Donny as he came to pick up another load of yetis. 'Once it's done, then there won't be any need for the other yetis to come.'

Donny shook his head seriously. 'The Ministry won't hold a meeting until all members are present.'

'How long will that be?' I asked nervously. 'How many yetis are we talking about here? Ten? Twenty?'

Donny shrugged, 'Around a hundred.'

100 x yeti stink!?

This is not good . . .

Monday 6th July

At lunchtime Mark herded us into an empty classroom like sheep.

He stood on a chair and shouted, 'Thank you all for coming, and for agreeing to be part of the USP: the Ultimate School Prank society!'

Hats off to Mark – he's done a stellar job of recruiting for the USP! There were loads of kids from my year there – even some of the cool kids from the older years too.

Somehow word had got out that it was me who smashed in the water pipe and got the school closed down last week. Honestly, I felt a bit of a fraud as people slapped me on the back and shook my hand. There's no way I can tell them the truth – that it was goth girl Red who'd pulled the pipe apart with the power of her mind.

When people asked me how I did it, I just said, 'A true legend never reveals his secrets.'

'We're here today to work as a team,' Mark said proudly. 'A team that is 100 per cent committed to pulling off the ultimate school prank. Your mission, should you choose to accept it, is to go away and think of a USP. Try them out on your kid sisters, do research on the Internet – do whatever you need to do. We'll meet back here every day until the end of term. Whoever comes up with the best prank will go down in the history books!'

HISTORY OF best PRANKS ever

A huge cheer erupted around the classroom but I felt numb. As exciting as the USP is, my heart just isn't in it. Is it wrong that I care more about yetis than I do about trashing my own school?

Am I sick?

Another yeti turned up while we were eating dinner tonight. It was Dad's turn to drive him to the zoo. 'I'll be fumigating the car for the next year,' he complained.

'Just another day of Feral madness,' Grace muttered as she left the dining table.

She's right. I don't even bat an eyelid at this kind of craziness any more!

Wednesday 8th July

The last two days have sucked more than a hungry leech for these five reasons:

1   Mark has cornered me a billion times and asked me what my ideas are for the USP.

2   Yetis are still appearing on my doorstep – but not all of them are here so we still can't have a Ministry meeting.

3   Natty ate my secret stash of bacon crisps.

4   Grace slammed a door so violently my framed snakeskin fell off my bedroom wall and smashed.

5 We still have no idea where Ant is keeping Bert.

Am too tired to write any more. Will report back tomorrow.

Friday 10th July

One very important thing has happened since I last wrote.

The moon is full. For most people, a full moon means nothing more than a chance to point up at the sky, eat a midnight feast and joke about werewolves.

But werewolves are not a joke. I live with five ex-werewolves, remember!

I was woken up this morning by the sound of Grace slamming her bedroom door and screaming, 'If you expect me to leave the house when my ear hair is this bad, then you can think again!'

Then Mum shouted at her for a while, and Grace shouted back from behind her closed bedroom door.

GET ME OUT OF HERE!!!!

Honestly, I couldn't get to school fast enough.

'Up all night with your pet frog, Sammy?' Mark asked when he saw the bags under my eyes.

I looked at him, confused. 'I don't have a pet . . .'

'Thought any more about the USP?' Mark grinned.

I shook my head.

'Honestly, Sammy,' Mark said, annoyed. 'Sometimes I think you live on another planet.'

Er, no, Mark. I don't live on another planet – I live in a house where yetis turn up at the front door. So excuse me if we're not on the same wavelength!

I bet if I gave it two minutes' thought, I'd come up with the most epic USP ever known to man. Plus I have a little sister who's perfect for trying stuff out on.

Stink bombs? Water balloons? Whoopee cushions? Swapping sugar for salt? Cling film over the toilet seat?

In fact, I've had an idea, and it's pretty awesome. All I need is an empty bucket and a whole load of water . . .

11 P.M.

Right, I'm taking a night off from weirdness and living the life of a normal kid.

USP practice #Take1

I've left Natty's bedroom door ajar and carefully placed a bucket of ice-cold water on top of it. As soon as she opens the door in the morning, the bucket will fall down and give her a drenching!

I'm sleeping on the landing so I can be here to witness the carnage first-hand.

It's going to be epic!

Saturday 11th July

'SAMMY FERAL, I HATE
YOU!!!!' bellowed Natty.

The USP practice totally,
totally worked.

As soon as Natty opened
her bedroom door, the water
bucket crashed down and
SOAKED her!

Hahahahaha!!!

Grace came out on to
the landing to see what
all the fuss was about.
She rolled her eyes

before quickly clamping her hands over her ears to hide the ear hair.

I could not stop laughing at the sight of Natty drenched in water! Mum, however, did not see the funny side. 'Practical jokes are not amusing!'

Oh yes, they are!

Natty hugged Mum, pretending to be upset, but I could see her secretly smiling. Mum shouted at me, 'Don't think you'll be spending the day Backstage with your friends and the yetis.'

I stopped laughing. 'But today's Saturday, Mum. Donny needs me!'

'Nope. You should know not to play practical jokes on your sister, Sammy. You're not going Backstage all day. You can help Seb at the penguin enclosure.'

Oh no! I know what that means . . .

'He needs someone to dress up as a giant penguin and pose for pictures – that's what you'll be doing today!'

'But, Mum . . .'

'No buts, Sammy. You'll do as you're told!'

NOT FAIR!

So that's how I ended up dressed in a giant penguin suit. Every screaming, snotty, squealing kid in the zoo wanted to stand next to me, hold my hand and have their photo taken. I was almost more popular than the real-life penguins!

OH, THE SHAME!

The day was mostly a sardine slushie of boredom as I waved at the crowds and waddled towards the nearest camera flash. It was getting near the end of the afternoon, and I was stifling my groans as yet another kid tugged on my flightless wings, when something caught my eye.

There was a spindly, insect-like figure walking slowly past the penguin beach. He was turned away from me and I couldn't see his face, but he clenched his fists as he walked and his arm muscles twitched like a grasshopper about to spring. The lanky figure had black hair and wore a black vest with army combat trousers.

My stomach tightened – I had a fishy hunch that it was Ant.

Ant, weirdo-boy, here in my zoo! You didn't need to be a detective to figure out he must be up to no good.

I decided to follow him . . .

But trying to be inconspicuous when you're dressed as a giant penguin is harder than hiding a yeti in a shoebox.

What choice did I have?

I waddled away quickly, the sound of disappointed children erupting behind me as I made my hasty escape. As soon as I was out of the penguin beach, I saw the black-haired figure turn the corner by the parrot cages. I shuffled closer, pressed my back against the blue-winged macaw's skyscraping enclosure and peered around the corner. Through my penguin mask I could see the gangly figure slipping out of sight – he was heading towards the tigers.

A crowd of children with party hats pointed and laughed at me. I ignored them and carried on . . .

I bit my lip as I waddled forward slowly, as if that would make me harder to spot . . .

The spindly, spider-like figure kept going, looking around suspiciously from left to right.

My heart lurched as he ground to a halt. Then he turned around and looked straight at me!

I reached out a wing and pulled in the nearest child I could see. I started waving at the crowd and the child looked up at me in confusion. My racing heart slowed down as I realized the figure had carried on – he obviously didn't know I was following him.

Phew! Lucky escape.

I was off again.

I waddled behind the boy, keeping a safe

distance. I followed him past the homes of Khan the Sumatran tiger, the spider monkeys, the pygmy hippos, the Galapagos tortoises and on towards the amphibian house. I lurked behind a refreshment stand as I watched him disappear into the amphibian house.

It had to be Ant. Had to be. Slowly I left the safety of the refreshment stand and wobbled towards the door. I peered into the gloom.

He was standing in front of the Amazon horned-frog tank, staring into its emptiness. I watched as he reached into his pocket and pulled something out. He placed it by the tank window. Then he looked around and stared straight at me with piercing violet eyes.

There was no point trying to hide. I was dressed as a giant penguin. I bravely pulled the penguin mask off. 'Can I help you?' I asked loudly.

He slowly walked towards me. 'I'm looking for Donny.'

He was taller than me, and his angular, bony face reminded me of an angry worker ant charging into battle. 'There's no one here called Donny,' I lied. He came closer, and in the half-light of the amphibian house his eyes glowed fierce purple. It was the strangest thing I'd ever seen – no way could he pass for normal. He was a total weirdo, for sure.

'Well, if you see him, tell him I said hi.' And then he brushed past me. It was the smallest of touches, but it sent me spinning off my flippers on to the floor. By the time I'd pulled myself up, Ant was long gone.

I looked over at the wish frog's empty tank. There was a letter propped up against it. Addressed to the wish frog.

I put my mask back on and ran Backstage

as fast as I could. I didn't
care if Mum saw me
and shouted at me
for abandoning my
penguin duties. This
was serious!

There were
dozens of yetis
milling about
Backstage. I steered
my giant penguin suit
through the crowd and

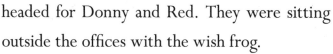

headed for Donny and Red. They were sitting
outside the offices with the wish frog.

'I've just seen Ant,' I said, panting. 'He left
this.'

Red stifled a laugh at my costume as I held
out the letter.

'Open it,' the wish frog croaked at Donny.
Donny tore the letter open and read:

Dear Wish Frog,

My plan to kidnap Bert has led me straight to you. You see, I've been looking for you for years. I'd almost given up hope of ever finding you when I heard a rumour that Genghis the death worm knew where you were hiding. Then I came up with a plan to kidnap Bert, Genghis's best friend. I knew that with Bert in peril, Genghis would come straight to you.

Now I know where you are, I suppose you must be wondering why I haven't come for you by now . . . I'm not stupid – I know I could never force you to grant my wishes. I knew you'd need some . . . persuading.

I won't give Bert back until I have what I want.

A wish. If you don't grant me my wish, Bert will never be seen alive again.

Meet me at the zoo gates at sundown in three days' time.

Ant

The wish frog lowered his eyes to the ground and blinked slowly. 'It's all my fault.'

'Don't blame yourself.' Donny screwed up his eyes eyes seriously. 'Ant is out of control. First he kidnaps Bert and then blackmails you – what next?'

'What do you think he wants to wish for?' I said anxiously.

Red shook her head. 'Whatever it is, we can't allow it to come true.'

'We can't wait any longer!' I said in Yeti, turning to Jane, Bob and Sid, who were looking on. *'We need to hold a Ministry meeting!'*

'The rules of the Ministry strictly forbid it,' Sid said gravely.

I pleaded. *'But we only have three days! How many more yetis are we waiting for?'*

'It's just Norman.' Jane shook her head. *'He's always late! Maybe just this once we could go ahead . . .'*

A rumble of fear, anger and confusion swept over the yetis. *'What's so bad about starting the meeting without Norman?'* I asked quietly.

'It is forbidden to hold a yeti meeting without all Ministry members present,' Jane said solemnly. *'If we did, then Norman could finish us all.'*

Wow, yetis really know how to be dramatic!

'How?'

'Two words for you, Sammy,' Jane said in a terrified voice. *'Yeti Snarl.'*

A Yeti Snarl?

'Go home and wait for Norman,' Jane said. *'That's all we can do. Wait.'*

So that's where I am now. I'm at home, waiting for Norman. He's still not arrived. And we only have three days! If we can't hold a meeting and can't rescue Bert, then Ant will finish him off. But if we hold a yeti meeting without Norman, Norman might come and finish us off!

This is bad, it's really, really bad . . .

Sunday 12th July

Two days until the fatal sunset showdown

Mum had me on penguin duty again today. She didn't care that I needed to wait at home for Norman. 'Norman will just have to find his own way to the zoo,' she said.

But Norman hasn't shown his fuzzy muzzle yet. All day long, I've posed for photo after stupid photo in my penguin suit, all the time looking out of the corner of my eye for a wandering yeti. After an entire day nearly boiling to death in the penguin suit, I finally came back home. But there's no sign of Norman here either.

11 P.M.

I can't sleep. Norman still hasn't arrived. I think we should just risk it and hold a Ministry of Yetis meeting without him. I'm sure he'd understand, wouldn't he? And if he doesn't, how bad can a Yeti Snarl really be?

11.55 P.M.

Jump on the party bus and dance like a spider monkey!

NORMAN IS HERE!!!

He's currently stuffing his face with lettuce — he's mega-hungry after his long journey.

'Can't you eat on the move?' I asked him. *'We really, really need to get you to the zoo.'*

Thankfully it's pitch black outside so no one can see me walking down the street with an enormous yeti munching on lettuce.

Donny yawned and rubbed his eyes as he opened the zoo gates for us. *'It's good to finally meet you, Norman.'* His Yeti is coming along really well.

Norman shook Donny's hand. *'Sorry it's taken me a while. I've been living in the Australian outback these past few years – it's been a bit of a long journey.'*

'I'll take Norman Backstage,' Donny told me. 'He needs to get some rest before we hold the meeting.'

'I'll be back at the zoo before school tomorrow,' I told him.

The meeting is in a few hours' time. I'd better get some zzzzzzzzz . . .

Monday 13th July
One day until the fatal sunset showdown

It was still dark when I walked through the zoo this morning. Bats, bush rats and the other nocturnal animals watched me wide-eyed as I yawned my way to the Backstage gates.

The Backstage yard was ram-packed with lumbering yetis. They were standing, elbow to elbow, in a perfect circle. 'They're ready to start the meeting as soon as the cock crows,' Donny told me as I pushed my way into the circle.

Genghis wriggled in next to me.

'Is this how it's always done?' I asked him.

'Oh sure,' he spat. *'Just come on over and interrogate me for information, Sammy. No "How are you?" or "Know any new nursery rhymes?"'*

Why does Genghis have to be such a crank?

'I'd rather we talked about the Ministry of Yetis,' I grumped back.

Genghis grudgingly told me everything I needed to know about the Ministry of Yetis (or M.O.Y. as they call it) – who's in it and how the meetings work. Here's a summary:

✱ M.O.Y. is made up of the most important yetis in the world

✱ Each yeti is voted into the M.O.Y.

✱ The M.O.Y. is the yeti equivalent of the humans' United Nations (whatever that is).

✱ Every member of the Ministry must be present for there to be a meeting.

✱ If a Ministry meeting goes ahead without
a member, then that missing member has
the right to inflict the Yeti Snarl.

'What is the Yeti Snarl?' I asked, curious.

'Sammy,' Genghis said, turning towards me
seriously. I quickly looked at the ground. *'You
know how much I hate humans . . .'* Oh, here we go.
'But as far as humans go, you're all right.' I nearly
keeled over in shock! That was the closest thing
to a compliment I'd ever heard from Genghis!
*'And for that reason, I hope you never find out what a
Yeti Snarl is.'*

Yeti Snarl = my new obsession. I HATE not
knowing what something is! As I opened my
mouth to ask more, Donny dragged a chair into
the middle of the circle. He stood on the chair
and shouted in Yeti, *'Thank you all for coming.
Murgo bimlo burgo.'*

Donny's Yeti still needs a LOT of work.

'Nonlo, rescue Bert. Huglo, no time to waste. Shimli, bimli, must plan,' he stuttered.

Grumbles rumbled through the circle as Donny tried to speak again. But before Donny could embarrass himself any more Jane stepped forward.

'We all know that Ant won't hand Bert back to us

unless we give him the wish frog. But the wish frog is the last of his kind. We need to protect him,' she said.

A murmur of agreement swept around the yard. I felt something hop on to my shoulder and looked down to see the wish frog shaking his head angrily. 'They still don't get it,' he croaked. 'Even if I wasn't the last of my kind, I wouldn't agree to grant wishes for Ant.'

'As is the yeti way,' Jane shouted – taking control of the meeting from Donny, *'each Ministry member should put forward their ideas, and then we will vote for the best one!'*

The next part of the meeting went on for hours. My stomach was grumbling, my feet were aching and my head was seriously throbbing from having to listen to dozens of yeti voices debating and arguing about their ideas. And, for the record, most yeti ideas are stupider than a mongoose on a skateboard.

After a complicated round of voting, a plan

was agreed. The plan is so stupid I can't even bring myself to write it down. It will never work. Ever.

'I'm not happy,' the wish frog informed me angrily. 'No innocent frogs should be hurt!'

I've got a bad feeling about tomorrow night. No way is the plan going to work. But if a whole Ministry of Yetis can't think of anything else, what hope do we have?

Tuesday 14th July
The day of the fatal sunset showdown

Ant's letter had told us to meet him at the zoo gates at sundown.

As soon as the zoo was empty of visitors, we took our positions. Jane, Norman, Sid and the others hid behind the ticket office, behind trees and behind any other large object they could find.

Donny and I crouched behind a rubbish bin.

'I've got the frog,' Donny told me nervously. He held up another Amazon horned frog, which blinked lazily and flicked out its tongue.

'Poor little guy,' I whispered. 'He has no idea what's about to happen.'

The wish frog stuck his head out of Donny's jacket pocket. 'Trust me, Sammy, you don't need to feel sorry for this one. He's the laziest, grumpiest, toad-looking, sorry excuse for a—'

'I thought you said you didn't want any innocent frogs hurt,' I pointed out.

'Hmmmm,' the wish frog muttered. 'I'd forgotten about that one.'

'Any sign of Ant?' Red asked, strolling up to us. 'I've left the worm Backstage. We've got enough to worry about this evening without spit-face in the mix.'

'Good call,' Donny agreed. 'No sign of Ant yet. Or Bert.' Red took the decoy frog from Donny and placed him by the gates . . . ready for Ant to scoop up.

We waited for ages. Time ticked by and the

sounds of the zoo animals rang in my ears as we waited and waited. Just as I was about to give up hope, a rake-thin boy climbed over the zoo gates and hurried towards us like a praying mantis scuttling towards its prey.

Ant.

He looked around suspiciously before spotting the frog sitting patiently on the ground. I held my breath as he squinted at it.

'Where's Bert?' the wish frog whispered in my ear.

Ant bent down, took one look at the frog and shook his head.

'Arghhhhh!!' came a terrible sound from a nearby tree.

Jane leaped out of hiding and stormed towards Ant, rage painted on her furry face. *'You took Bert! Prepare to die!'*

This was not part of the plan! As Jane lunged at Ant, he calmly stretched out his arm as if stopping a small child from coming closer. Jane crashed into his open palm like a clap of thunder. The sound echoed around the zoo.

Jane rose to her feet, ready to strike again. I watched in horror as all around me yetis burst out of hiding.

'*What about the plan?*' I cried in Yeti. But no one was listening. The sight of Ant, the lanky boy who had kidnapped their chief, had driven them wild. They wanted his blood! Every yeti thumped towards him. They lunged, charged and pushed, ready to tear him to shreds with their terrible claws. My heart nearly exploded in panic as I watched the horrible scene unfold.

The bigger the yeti, the harder they fell. And Ant, the gangling, lanky teenager who looked less powerful than a measly stick insect, overpowered each yeti without even breaking into a sweat.

'*HELP! STOP! SOS!!!*'

Donny screamed in Yeti while Red tried to use her powers to hold the crazed yetis back. The wish frog froze in fear at the war that was raging around us. Everyone was losing it!

But there was one person who stayed as calm

as a two-toed sloth on a Sunday – Ant. He batted the beasts away as if they were flies. A flick of his wrist sent Norman crashing to the ground. A backwards nudge of his elbow had Sid flying through the air and crashing into the ticket desk. He laughed. 'You think you can overpower me?'

'Stop!' Donny shouted, getting to his feet.

Ant's purple eyes lit up at the sight of Donny.

'*Stop!*' I yelled in Yeti. The yetis growled and curled their lips, standing poised to attack again.

'Donny, we meet again,' Ant snarled. 'And this must be Red. I've heard so much about you. You know, I could use talent like yours. If you ever want to come and work for someone with real power . . .'

'I'd never work for you,' Red snapped back. 'I'd rather die a thousand painful deaths.'

'That can easily be arranged.' Ant grinned.

'Where's Bert?' Donny demanded.

'He's somewhere you'll never find him. I was ready to give him back to you, in a fair exchange, but we all know that this sorry excuse for a frog has no more power than a common tadpole. I know you have the wish frog – give him to me!'

I took a step forward and shouted, 'Even if we did have him, the wish frog would never work for you!'

Ant locked me in a cold stare, his eyes narrowed like those of a jaguar eyeing up prey. Every muscle in my body tensed as he paced slowly towards me.

'You . . .' He smiled at me. 'You've had your chance to play nice. Next time I won't be so kind.'

In the blink of an eye he was up and over the zoo gate. Yetis scrambled towards him, ready to give chase. *'No!'* I shouted. *'If you kill him, we'll never find Bert!'*

'We should have torn his head off!' Jane cried.

Red looked at Donny in horror. I'd never seen her look so scared. 'If an army of yetis can't overpower him, then what can we do?' she said.

'There's more than one way to win a war,' Donny said calmly. 'When we meet Ant again, we'll be ready!'

Wednesday 15th July

I was sweeping out the baboons this evening when Dad wandered past. 'This came in the post for you today.' He handed me a brown envelope with my name on the front. 'There's no stamp — it must have been hand-delivered.'

The broom fell from my hands as I grabbed the letter. I'd have bet a zoo-ful of black widow spiders that I knew who it was from. Dad shouted after me as I bolted away from him with the letter in my hands.

I hardly recognized Backstage as I burst through the gates. The yetis had been hard at work. The yard looked like a Bigfoot paradise.

They'd constructed fake caves out of old bits of metal and sheets of plastic. They'd built fire pits to cook vegetables on and the stench of rotten cabbage made my stomach spasm in disgust. I looked around in wonder, nearly forgetting that the world was about to end.

'Sammy!' Donny greeted me, weaving through the crowds of yetis towards me.

I held the envelope out without a word.

Donny threw me a worried look. 'Read it.'

The wish frog hopped on to Red's shoulder and Donny came in closer as I ripped open the envelope.

Sammy Feral,

If you're so very smart, then I'd like to see how you get yourself out of this one.

What does a yeti have at the end of his big foot?

Bert is now missing one of these precious digits.

I am not joking when I tell you that Bert's life is in peril, and there's only one way you can save him . . . he's small, ugly and grants wishes. ——— ———

You have ten days.

Ant

There was something else inside the envelope.

'No!' The wish frog trembled as I held up Bert's chopped-off toe. 'How could he?'

Red looked around, worried. 'Sammy, quick, put that away before . . .'

'*That looks like . . .*' Jane stopped mid-sentence as she saw me hurriedly stuff Bert's big toe back out of sight. She snatched the envelope from my hands and peered in anxiously. *'No!'*

She let out a wail like a baby elephant torn away from its mother.

'*Jane,*' Donny warned. '*Be quiet or you'll start snarling.*'

My eyebrows rose. 'Snarl?'

Jane pulled herself together. *'I'm sorry. It's just the sight of poor Bert's toe . . . makes me realize just how much I still . . .'*

'It's OK, Jane.' I patted her hairy arm. *'We're going to bring him home before Ant can chop anything else off, I promise.'*

Jane's eyes pleaded with me. *'How?'*

I looked around at the blank faces of Donny, Red, Jane and the wish frog.

'I don't know,' I admitted. *'But we have ten days to figure it out.'*

Thursday 16th July
9 days until rendezvous

Wow, if I was under any more pressure then my head would explode like a cheap balloon!

I'm under SERIOUS stress at school trying to brainstorm pranks. And the situation at the zoo hasn't got any better – we still don't know how we're going to rescue Bert.

'I just wish there was something I could do to help,' the wish frog said sadly this evening.

The obvious thing would be for him to just grant us a wish that would make this whole stress soufflé a lot easier to swallow.

'You seem worried, Sammy,' the frog said thoughtfully.

Ya think!!

'I've just got a lot going on at the moment – what with Bert, and everything at school.' He looked at me blankly. 'The kids at school want me to pull off the ultimate school prank, but I just don't know how.'

'Now *that* I can help with.' The wish frog beamed.

So that's when I agreed to take the wish frog into school tomorrow. He's going to help me pull off the ultimate USP . . .

Friday 17th July
8 days until rendezvous

Freedom!! School's out for summer!

I'd be as happy as a banana-boating bat if I didn't have the case of the missing yeti hanging over me. Let's just say that the wish frog is officially the coolest little dude to ever splash in a puddle. In fact, I'd go so far as to say the wish frog is my new BFF. Does having a frog for a best friend make me a freak?

Who cares? I was carried away by the freak train a loooong time ago! The wish frog and I stayed up late last night fine-tuning our epic prank plan.

The morning passed by quickly enough – everyone was way too excited about the holidays to concentrate much in class. I'm pretty sure the teachers felt the same way – they didn't even care that no one was listening. Of course, the usual pranks were played – whoopee cushions, silly string, etc.

'I've got the USP,' I said confidently to Mark. I pulled the wish frog out of my pocket.

He looked at me. 'You brought your pet frog to school?'

'He's part of the prank,' I told him. 'I've been using him to practise ventriloquism.'

'Ven-what?' Mark asked.

'Just meet me outside Mr Lewis's classroom at lunchtime – this is going to be epic!'

Mark spread the word to the rest of the USP Society. When lunchtime came around, we gathered outside Mr Lewis's classroom. 'Time to rock 'n' roll,' I whispered to the wish frog.

I carefully took him out of my pocket and put him on the floor. He hopped into the empty classroom, where Mr Lewis was reading the paper and eating his sandwiches.

I covered my mouth with my hands, so no one could see my lips.

That's when the wish frog started to speak. 'Excuse me, sir,' he croaked. Mr Lewis looked up, startled, but didn't see the wish frog. He looked back down at his paper. 'Excuse me!' the wish frog croaked louder, hopping on to the table opposite Mr Lewis's desk.

Mr Lewis dropped his sandwich and looked at the wish frog in horror.

Everyone around me started sniggering. 'He thinks the frog's speaking!' Mark giggled. 'This is hysterical!'

The wish frog lifted one foot in the air, as if making an interesting point, and spoke again. 'I wonder if I could trouble you for some maths advice?'

Mr Lewis went as white as a polar bear and got shakily to his feet. 'Did you just speak? But you're a . . . a . . . frog!'

'I was wondering,' the wish frog said loudly, 'if I catch two flies for breakfast, three stick insects for lunch and big juicy moth for dinner, just how many insects will I eat in a week?'

Mr Lewis didn't hang about to hear any more. He ran from the room screaming. We could hear him charging down the school corridor, swearing and crying, 'I've gone mad!'

Everyone congratulated me. 'That was amazing, Sammy!'

'Where did you learn how to do that?' Mark beamed. 'It really sounded like it was the frog speaking.'

'I've spent a lot of time practising,' I lied.

The rest of the day was a blur of celebration and people re-telling the story of the talking frog. The wish frog is staying at my house this evening. I've made a little bed for him out of an old soap dish, some mud and leaves from the garden.

If I don't think about Bert, then I'm really happy. Today was a good day, and that can only mean one thing . . . tomorrow is going to be weird.

Saturday 18th July
7 days until rendezvous

Feral family breakfast time = total chaos!

If I wanted any more drama, I'd wear a suit of raw meat and breakdance through the tiger den!

'I've written a four-page letter about why I should have another hamster,' Natty announced. 'I've used my best joined-up writing and my pink pen.'

'You can't have another hamster,' Dad said firmly, brewing the morning coffee. 'You ate the last one.'

'We're going on holiday,' Mum interrupted

loudly. Everyone fell silent and Natty dropped her letter to the floor.

'Can I come too?' asked the wish frog. 'Where are you going?'

'We're going to visit my parents on the Galapagos Islands,' Dad said to the wish frog. Most people's parents might think it's weird that their kids are hanging out with talking frogs, but not mine.

Grace threw her hands up in the air dramatically. 'Great! Just when life couldn't get any worse, you're taking me away from everything I know and plonking me on an island of volcanic rock!'

'Do we have to go?' I complained.

Now is not the time to be going on holiday. I've got a kidnapped Yeti Chief and an endangered wish frog to worry about!

Mum sighed. 'Sammy, you've always wanted to go to the Galapagos Islands.'

'You should be careful what you wish for!' the wish frog said smugly.

Of course I want to go to the Galapagos Islands, but how can I tell Mum that I need to stay here without telling her the truth about Bert? If she knew what I'd got myself mixed up in then she'd be buying me a one-way ticket and keeping me as far away from the zoo as possible!

I got myself a bowl of cereal, and as I poured in the milk the wish frog leaped into the bowl and started to splash about. 'Ah, nothing like a morning milk wash!'

Seriously, can I not even have a bowl of cereal without something weird happening?

After I wolfed down breakfast and argued a bit more about going away on holiday, the wish frog jumped into my pocket and we left for the zoo.

I quickly did my morning chores: clearing spat-out bones from the vulture enclosure, feeding the alligators and unpacking a delivery of frozen mice. As I headed for Backstage, the noise erupting from behind the gates made me dread what I was about to find.

'What is going on?' I shouted as I closed the gates behind me. I looked around in horror at the scene of absolute carnage!

Upturned cages and ripped-apart fences scattered the yard. Half-chewed carrots rotted in the fire pits and the stench of dozens of yetis was almost too much to bear. Donny waved at me from the other side of the yard, then dodged past two yetis about to have a punch-up and headed over. 'Yetis are solitary creatures by nature,' he said calmly. 'They don't like being cooped up like this, having to compete for space.'

'HE STOLE MY CABBAGE!' screamed Jane as she ran towards me, pointing at Sid. 'I turned my back for one minute!'

Genghis wriggled up to us. 'If we don't do something soon,' he said in perfect English (Max must have been working him hard), 'then it won't just be Bert that's in trouble. Your whole zoo will be smashed down!'

'We need an emergency meeting!' I yelled at the yetis.

'The Ministry will only meet in the morning,' Jane growled at me.

'First thing tomorrow,' I told her. 'Tell every yeti here to come prepared! Tomorrow we're going to decide our battle plan!'

Sunday 19th July
6 days until rendezvous

There was no time for Donny's bad Yeti-speak at sunrise. So I dragged the chair into the middle of the yeti circle and spoke instead. *'Thank you all for coming. Two heads are better than one, and we have a hundred yeti heads Backstage at the moment. No one leaves until we have a plan!'*

Who knew I could be so bossy? I must get it from Mum.

Red watched me, looking furious, and Donny just stood there, mouth agape. Genghis writhed up to the foot of the chair as if he was my side-kick, and the wish frog hopped on to his head.

Everyone watched me silently, and I spoke again. *'There's no way we can use brute strength to battle Ant. That much is obvious. Instead we need to outsmart him, and use whatever other powers we have to bring him down!'* Everyone nodded and mumbled in agreement.

'Red, we can use your telekinesis,' I said to her. 'And, Genghis, that spit will come in handy. Maybe my CSC can help somehow. *And everyone else —'* I said this bit in Yeti — *'I know that yetis have some kind of power — you might not like using it, or even talking about it. But now is not the time to be shy. The last ever wish frog needs our protection, and Bert needs to be rescued. Now is the time to stand up and FIGHT!'*

I punched the air with my fist, and to my surprise everyone else did the same. A loud cheer rung out from the crowd and I felt myself beam with pride. Maybe, just maybe, we could do this . . .

Jane stepped forward. *'The Yeti Snarl,'* she said solemnly. *'Brothers, sisters —'* she looked around at the other yetis — *'we have six days until we meet with Ant. Six days to come together, to hone our snarl and prepare for battle!'* Again a loud cheer rang out and everyone clapped their giant paws in applause.

'And so,' I concluded, *'I propose that we meet back here every day at sunrise for the next six days. Every day we shall report back on our progress, share our ideas and refine our plan. We're going to make this work. We're going to bring Bert home.'*

A loud and clear *'Yes!'* rang out in Yeti. My ears thundered and my heart beat with pride.

I climbed down off the chair and dragged it back into the office.

'Good work, Sammy,' Donny said, as he and Red followed me.

'Thanks,' I said. 'But it won't mean anything if we don't find Bert.'

There was a tap on the Backstage office door. Jane was ducking her head and trying to come into the office – she'd crash through the roof if she wasn't careful. *'Sammy?'*

'Wait there – I'll come out,' I said, walking over to her and saving the office roof from certain destruction. *'What's up?'*

'We've decided to make you an honorary member of the Ministry of Yetis,' she said shyly. *'You really impressed us back there – it was as if you were one of us. It almost reminded me of Bert . . . your way with words, your natural charisma and authority. It's like I look at you and see him.'* She fluttered her eyelashes at me and gave me the kind of smile I've seen Grace give to Max before.

Did I want to be an honorary Yeti Ministry member – of course!

Did I want Jane to be my yeti girlfriend – no way!

'That really is an honour,' I replied. 'I accept, thank you.' Jane leaned forward and just as I thought she was going in for a sloppy yeti snog I stepped back quickly.

'Er, better get to work — lots to think about!' I quickly shut the office door. 'Did you see that?' I asked Donny and Red.

Red looked like she was about to explode with laughter. 'Your first kiss?'

I ignored Red and her stupid comment. 'They've asked me to be a member of the Ministry of Yetis.'

Donny's face fell to the floor and I felt as if I'd punched him in the gut.

'Congratulations.' He smiled at me weakly. 'You deserve it. Looks like you don't need us any more, Sammy.'

He walked past me, into the other room where he keeps his pets, and closed the door.

'Donny, wait . . .'

'He's always wanted to join the Ministry of Yetis,' Red told me. 'I hope it means as much to you as it would do to him.' And then she left me.

Great, that's just what I need – Donny and Red in a sulk with me for something I didn't even want. Of course I still need them – what would I do without them?

Sure, they can't speak Yeti or Death Worm, but there are other things they help out with . . .

Aren't there?

Monday 20th July
5 days until rendezvous

I was at the zoo before sunrise, standing on a chair again and addressing the circle of yetis.

'Jane, can you give me an update on your Yeti Snarl practice?' I asked, straight to the point.

She looked around sheepishly. *'We haven't released a snarl yet. The thing is, Sammy, a Yeti Snarl can be lethal, and when yetis get together and snarl as one, the effect can be catastrophic.'*

'Bert isn't going to rescue himself,' I said loudly, in my best teacher voice. *'You need to practise. Tomorrow at the meeting, I want a proper update.'*

The yetis looked pretty annoyed with me – as if I cared! I was trying to help them!

After the meeting Donny grabbed my arm and took me aside. 'Sammy, we need to talk.'

'I'm doing my best,' I told him. 'But if the yetis won't practise, then what can I . . . ?'

'That's not it. You're doing a great job,' he reassured me. Red came over and stood next to Donny. They exchanged a strange glance.

They were making me paranoid. 'What's going on?'

'We're moving on, kid,' Red replied. 'Got other places to go, people to see.'

Rewind! Er, what?

'You can't go!' I panicked. 'We haven't found Bert yet. We only have five days left and . . .'

'Sammy, I'm proud of you.' Donny put a hand on my shoulder. 'You've come such a long way from the boy I found open-mouthed about to be eaten by werewolves. You don't need us here at the zoo.'

'No, you're wrong,' I said, feeling like the world was crashing down around me. 'I need you.'

The wish frog hopped on to my shoulder. 'You've got me,' he croaked.

'Donny, *please.*'

He shook his head. 'Sorry, Sammy, you're on your own . . . I'll be in touch if I hear anything about where Ant might be keeping Bert.'

I didn't stay Backstage to watch Donny pack his bags and leave. I couldn't bear it. I thought that if I pretended it wasn't happening, then maybe it wouldn't, and he'd stay.

But I came Backstage this evening and Donny's pets, books and clothes have all gone – so have Red's. They've really gone. They've left me alone. I can't believe it.

Tuesday 21st July
4 days until rendezvous

Being without Donny and Red sucks more than a vampire bat at an all-you-can-eat bloody buffet.

The only good thing about my day was an exploding cabbage . . .

'We think it best that we show you the power of one Yeti Snarl,' Jane said nervously at the Ministry meeting this morning. *'Then you will have an idea of the power of a hundred snarls.'*

I stood on the chair in the centre of the circle, my shoulders slumped and the corners of my mouth nearly touching the floor. I'd been dying to find out what a Yeti Snarl was, but now I was about to, I couldn't care less.

What was the point of anything without Donny there?

Sid shuffled nervously into the centre of the circle with a stinking cabbage under his arm. He placed it by his feet and took a step back. *'Cover your ears,'* he warned me.

With my hands over my ears, I watched in horror as Sid's lips began to quiver and a horrible snarl sound escaped. He directed the snarl at the cabbage as if he was aiming a loaded gun. The cabbage began to shake. It lifted slightly from the ground, hovering in mid-air. The shaking grew more violent, and then it exploded.

Rotten cabbage leaves splattered all over me!

I wiped them from my face in shock. *'That's a Yeti Snarl?'* Sid nodded guiltily.

'If one yeti can make something explode, then what can a hundred yetis together do?' I asked.

'We can make things disappear,' Sid replied. *'We can snarl things out of existence, vaporize them into thin air.'*

No. Way.

The Yeti Snarl is a lot like Red's powers of telekinesis, only much, much deadlier. Kind of cool, but definitely kind of scary.

'Keep practising,' I told them, feeling my knees knock beneath me at the thought of a Yeti Snarl in my direction. *'And only practise on cabbages.'*

As the yetis left the circle and gathered into smaller practise groups, I pulled my phone out of my pocket and texted Donny:

I've seen a Yeti Snarl! Amaze! Definitely have a chance of beating Ant!

No reply from Donny yet . . .

LATER

I've texted Donny again:

> Mate, please come back.

Haven't heard from him. Maybe he hates me. I should never have accepted the honorary membership of the Ministry of Yetis.

Wednesday 22nd July
3 days until rendezvous

Making my way to the Ministry meeting this morning was like walking through a war zone.

Backstage is covered with cabbage mush. It squelched under my feet and smelt worse than hippo poo on a hot day!

'You gotta break me outta here,' the wish frog begged as I dragged a chair into the circle. 'I can't take much more. The Yeti Snarls are getting too close for comfort. I'm a chilled kinda guy, I like the easy life. But this here –' he pointed at two yetis hand in hand exploding a cabbage into smithereens – 'that could be me if I take one hop in the wrong direction!'

So the snarl practise isn't going well then. Cabbages should be disappearing, not exploding!

'We have made some improvement,' Sid told me at the meeting. *'Last night a group of us made half a cabbage disappear.'*

'Just keep practising – we have another three days,' I said, trying to sound confident.

But I'm not confident. Inside I'm as panicked as a porcupine on a tightrope.

Even if the yetis do manage to perfect their snarl, I still have no idea how we're going to use it to overpower Ant! We don't even know where he is!

This is the worst plan in the history of everything!

7 P.M.

If I didn't know as much about animals as I do,

197

then it would be easy to mistake Grace for a giant sloth. That girl has done nothing but mope since she broke up with Max. And just like you can track and predict a wild animal's movements, so I am learning to predict Grace's. I know from experience that I will always find her by the kitchen coffee machine in the morning, checking out her make-up in the zoo bathrooms at lunchtime and hanging around the penguins at feeding time, hoping to see Max.

I have learned to avoid all these areas at the times Grace will be there.

One place Grave never goes is the reptile house. So I was sitting by Beelzebub's tank, jotting down ideas for Bert's rescue mission:

✱ Parachute in.

✱ Get Red to levitate me in.

✱ Ride on a kangaroo as he hops in.

There's one obvious flaw to all my ideas. We don't know where 'in' is. What's the point of clever ideas if we don't know where to find Bert? I just can't think what else to do to track him down. How do you find someone that is trying so hard not to be found?

I looked up to see Max bounding towards me.

'And that,' he said proudly, dumping a leather-bound journal at my feet, 'is how you write a project on rare animals! Fingers crossed it's good enough to win me a place at the Royal College of Zoology.'

I flicked through the journal. Max had done a great job of writing up everything he'd learned, cleverly disguising the fact it was a Mongolian death worm he was studying and not a rare caramel Burmese python.

'What are you doing this afternoon?' he asked. 'Want to celebrate? We could watch some new tarantulas hatch, and then maybe hit the ice-cream stand by the penguins?'

'Maybe later,' I said, getting to my feet. 'I've got a project of my own to work on. It's not going so well. In fact, it's totally flawed.'

Max shrugged at me. 'Everything has its flaws. Projects, animals, people. Nothing is perfect, no matter how good and strong it might seem. Don't get hung up on flaws. Focus on the positives.'

My eyes widened as a light bulb flashed in my head. He was right. Everything has its flaws . . . even people . . . even super-strong people . . . even Ant.

'A fatal flaw,' I said quietly – an idea creeping into my head. . .

Ant's fatal flaw – that was the only way to bring him to his knees.

Now I just need to figure out what that flaw is, and then I need to find out where to find him!

Thursday 23rd July
2 days until rendezvous

He's back! He's back! He's back!

Red too – I'm even happy to see her miserable, racoon-eyed face! I saw Donny as soon as I came Backstage for the Ministry meeting at sunrise.

Red smiled. 'We know where Ant is keeping Bert.'

I nearly burst like an exploding cabbage. 'Where? How did you find out?'

'As you know, we put word out on the crypto-street some time ago that we were searching for Ant.' Donny shook his grey hair and grinned. 'But no one's come forward with any information that's been useful. Until yesterday . . .'

'That's what you've been doing?' My heart soared. 'Looking for Ant?'

'Of course.' Red smirked. 'You didn't think we'd abandon you completely, did you, kid?'

'We shouldn't have left like that,' Donny admitted. 'Of course we want to help rescue Bert.'

'So where is he?' Genghis asked with gut-wrenching hope. 'How did you find him?'

'Dr Lycan,' Donny answered.

Dr Lycan is an ex-werewolf who helped me find a cure for the werewolf virus. If it hadn't been for all Dr Lycan's old science journals, my family would still be walking around on all fours once a month. 'How did Dr Lycan know where Ant was?' I said.

'She saw Ant bulk-buying lettuces last week.

She knew we'd been looking for him, so she tipped us off.' Donny grinned again.

'We spent the last few nights staking out the shop where Dr Lycan spotted Ant, waiting for him to come back,' Red continued. 'Once we saw him, all we had to do was follow him back to his hideout.'

Donny leaned back on his heels, as casual as ever. 'Bert's being held at an old country mansion a few hours' drive away.'

'And that's where we'll attack?' I asked. 'In two days' time?'

Donny and Red exchanged a quick glance before flashing cunning smiles. 'We're not waiting, Sammy. We attack tomorrow.'

'Tomorrow?' Genghis spat with

surprise. Everyone jumped back to avoid the acid spray. 'That's too soon!'

'Genghis is right,' I agreed. 'The yeti army is looking pretty fierce, but I don't think cutting their training short by a day will go down well.'

'At the moment we have the element of surprise on our side,' Donny said seriously. 'If they're not ready tomorrow, then they never will be. We leave at dawn.'

So that's decided then.

Only one thing left to do – assemble the Ministry of Yetis to prepare for battle!

I stood on a chair in the middle of the circle, with Red and Donny either side of me. It felt good to be a team again. The wish frog sat on Genghis's head by Donny's feet, like an obedient Labrador.

Time to break the news.

We leave at dawn!' I declared, without any introduction.

The yetis exchanged nervous glances before
Sid called out, *'A day before schedule? So we have the
element of surprise on our side?'*

'That's right.' I tried to sound as positive as I

could – although inside I worried that Donny's plan was as stupid as an octopus on ice skates.

'Do we know where he is?' Jane asked.

I looked at Donny and Red. *'Yes. We leave at dawn!'*

There was a cheer from the crowd and a few of them punched the air and whooped with excitement. I was surprised how keen they were to get the battle under way.

Sid stepped forward. *'So, we know where we're going. And we know what we have to do as an army when we get there. But while we can break through Ant's defences, we'll need more than that to defeat him completely. That was your job, Sammy,'* he pointed out. *'What's the plan?'*

'I've given it a lot of thought,' I nodded. *'Ant is strong, sure. But everyone – even super-strong weirdos – has a fatal flaw. We need to play on this if we have any hope of defeating Ant.'* I quickly translated the conversation for Donny and Red.

'Interesting idea,' Donny said thoughtfully. 'What do you suppose Ant's fatal flaw is?'

'Greed,' I said simply. 'That's why he wants the wish frog to work for him. Greed – that's his weakness. That's how we'll destroy him.'

'I have a plan,' I announced. *'I'll fill you all in as we travel. Everyone has a part to play.* Wish Frog,' I turned down to look at the little guy I now call my friend, 'you know what you have to do?'

He gulped bravely. 'No decoy frogs this time.'

'That's right. It's all on you.'

Tomorrow is judgement day. I can't sleep – my mind is buzzing like a bee, questions going round and round. Will the yeti army need to fight to the death to defeat Ant? Will the wish frog escape unharmed? Will Bert finally be free? Will I still be alive to write in this diary tomorrow?

There's only one way to find out . . .

Friday 24th July
Day of the attack!

Operation: Yeti Rescue!

Mission: Save Bert the Yeti Chief

Hostage Location: Ant's mega-mansion

Enemy: Ant – weirdo with super-strength

Friendly Forces: Yeti army, Donny, Red, me, Genghis, Wish Frog

Transportation of Troops: Rented double-decker bus

Weapons: Red's telekinesis, my CSC, Yeti Snarl, Genghis's acid spit and death stare

It's 3 a.m., and we're travelling under the cover of darkness. I snuck out my bedroom window and climbed down the drainpipe before meeting our army at the zoo. Mum and Dad don't know where I am – they'd ground me forever if they did. I didn't have a chance to say goodbye – what if I never see them again?

We've spent the last hour in the bus going over and over the plan. 'Failing to prepare is preparing to fail,' the wish frog reminded us sensibly.

Everyone knows what they have to do. If it all goes wrong, then we tried our best.

My eyes are watering from the smell of so many yetis in a confined space. My stomach is doing somersaults. It's like I've been strapped to the wings of a mighty condor and I'm gliding over a mountaintop. I think I might be sick – it's the nerves, and the stench.

'We'll be there in ten!' Donny has just announced.

It's show time . . .

MUCH, MUCH LATER

From a distance, Ant's mansion looked like a castle. I dread to think who he had to beat up to get himself in there.

Donny parked the bus at the top of a long, long driveway. We filed off the bus and walked towards the mansion gates in silence. My heart raced as I looked around me at the army I was part of. The sight of so many yetis was breathtaking. They towered above me like skyscrapers, each one ready to do whatever it took – fight to the death, if necessary.

There was a security camera perched high on the iron gate. 'I'll take care of it,' Red muttered, before exploding it to dust with her telekinesis.

There were five other cameras along the way. Red took them all out. She blew up the security lights too, so Ant couldn't see us approach. We were in total darkness as we advanced towards the mansion. Nothing but the soft thud of yeti paws, the hoot of night owls and the nervous growls of my stomach sounded around us. Ant had no way of knowing we were approaching.

The element of surprise was still on our side.

Jane twitched her nose like a hungry dog. 'I

can smell him. His scent is faint, but he's definitely here.'

The lumbering yeti led us right up to the mansion. Up close, it was even more imposing. Stone turrets rose into the misty night and dozens of darkened window panes lined the moss-covered walls. Jane sniffed at the air and licked her lips as we approached.

Donny pointed up at the dark windows and whispered, 'He must be sound asleep.'

'Dreaming of world domination,' Genghis added in perfect English. Max really was a great teacher.

'Lift me up,' Donny instructed Red. She dutifully struggled to lift Donny high up in the air using her telekinesis. She concentrated hard as she moved Donny between windows. We all watched in hope and terror as Donny peered into the blackness of each room, and shook his head before moving on to the next. Donny rose higher and higher, spying into the rooms at the very top of the house. The higher he got, the more Red struggled to hold him.

'I can't hold him much longer,' Red grunted desperately.

At that moment Donny looked down, gave a thumbs up and nodded with excitement. She carefully lowered him back to the ground. 'He's in there.' Donny pointed to a small window at the top of the house. 'Fast asleep.'

'Phase one of the plan complete,' I said with relief. 'Enemy located. *Norman, you know what to do when we get in there?*' I said in Yeti. Norman nodded and gulped.

Donny moved through the army of yetis to reach the front door. *'Every one of you has sacrificed something to be here tonight,'* he said in perfect Yeti. *'No matter what happens, Bert will be proud.'*

With a breath to steady his nerves, Donny gave Red a nod. She clicked the mansion door lock open with a look. The door creaked on its hinges, swinging wide to reveal a grand hallway with a winding staircase. The mansion was humongous. 'It'll take weeks to search this place for Bert,' the wish frog whispered, sitting on my shoulder.

Jane took a giant yeti step into the hallway. *'He's definitely here.'*

'Quick.' Donny followed Jane into the house, and the long line of yetis trailed after him.

'I'll stand watch outside Ant's door,' Norman whispered as he broke away from the group. *'If he so much as stirs in his sleep, I'll let out the Call of the Yeti.'*

Jane's nose twitched like crazy as she followed Bert's scent through the entrance hall and down a dark corridor. She paused at a dingy stairwell. *'This must lead down to the cellars,'* she whispered.

Donny gulped. 'I'll lead the way.' He

slowly descended, each wooden step creaking underneath his weight. Jane followed close behind, Red, Genghis and I only a few steps back. Behind me was the rest of the yeti army. I could hear their deep growls and heavy breathing as the air filled with the tension of what was to come.

CRASH!!!

'Donny!' Red screamed loudly.

If the crash hadn't woken Ant, then Red's screaming surely would!

Disaster!

As Donny's foot landed on the next creaking stair a trap door had opened up. He'd fallen through the hole but managed to catch the edge of the ledge with his fingertips.

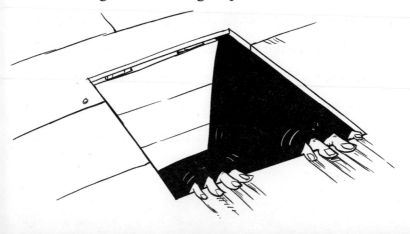

His legs kicked about in the darkness below, and just as he was about to lose his grip Jane bent down and lifted him back on to safe ground. 'The stairs,' Red hissed. 'They're booby-trapped!'

There was no way we were going to rescue Bert without a struggle – Ant had made sure of that.

We took every step as if it was our last. At any moment I was expecting Norman's deafening Yeti Call to warn us that Ant was on his way. We tiptoed on to each stair carefully, but we couldn't be careful enough.

Out of nowhere, a giant net fell on Jane, tangling her up. We all worked together to free her, desperate not to make a sound and let Ant know we were here.

'If I'd been on my own, I'd have been—'

Jane didn't finish what she was saying, as burning hot flames suddenly shot out at us from a crack in the wall. 'Hidden flamethrowers!' I whispered. 'We'll be lucky if we ever make it to the bottom of these stairs!'

Once the flamethrowers had been activated, they fired away around us. The heat was intense and my skin prickled with sweat. Somehow, we all managed to dodge the flames to reach the bottom of the stairs.

Just as I thought we'd made it safely, a rush of noise and a gush of air rushed in our direction. I clapped my hands over my ears at the sound of a hundred shrieking bats flapping towards us.

'*GET DOWN!!*' Donny shouted in Yeti.

I crouched down low, and I heard the creak of yeti knees as everyone behind me squatted down too. A huge colony of bats swooped over us, flapping their black wings and flying out into the night.

'Looks like Bert isn't the only one living down here,' Red commented.

'At least he hasn't been alone,' Genghis pointed out.

At last we reached the bottom of the stairs and stepped out into a giant murky cellar. The air stank of mould and you could hear trickles of water running down the moist walls. The yetis had to stoop low as they entered. Rats scuttled around our feet and I had to shuffle my legs like a disco dancer to stop them climbing up me!

There was a loud groan in the darkness.

Bert?

'Bert!' Genghis shouted with glee. *'I've found you!'*

As my eyes adjusted to the gloom I could just about make out the giant shape of Bert sitting propped against the rough wall. His ankles were shackled to the ground and around him lay the remains of half-eaten cabbages.

'*Genghis!*' Bert smiled. '*Donny . . . Jane?*'

'*Oh, my love!*' Jane shouted, rushing towards
him.

There was a loud creak from the staircase.
Ant was on his way down!

Had he slipped past Norman? Had Norman
failed to make the Call of the Yeti? Was Norman
dead?!

No time for questions.

'Everyone, hide away in the darkness,' I growled.
'Remember the plan!'

Donny, Red, Genghis and the yetis scuttled
away into the shadows, pressing their backs
against the nearest wall and holding their
breath.

'What's going on?' Bert asked desperately.

'We're here to help you,' I whispered in Yeti to
Bert. *'Trust me. And play along.'*

Bert nodded and a flicker
of understanding sparkled
in his bulging yeti eyes.

My heart beat so
loudly I was sure Ant
would hear it as he
came down the stairs
towards me. In one
hand he held an old-
fashioned lantern that

lit up his wicked grin, in the other he grasped Norman's thick furry neck.

As Ant entered the sprawling cellar, Norman opened his mouth to speak. Ant squeezed his throat tighter and Norman's eyes bulged in his skull. 'Look what I found lurking outside my bedroom,' came Ant's sinister voice in the darkness. 'I wasn't expecting you until tomorrow night. How did you find me? I thought I'd covered all my tracks.'

'We're here alone,' I lied, avoiding the question. 'Norman and me. We've brought you the wish frog.' The wish frog dutifully leaped from my shoulder and sat on my open palm. 'We've come to work for you.'

I held my breath. There was every chance that Ant had seen me come into the house with a yeti army close behind. There was every chance he could smell them, every chance he knew I was lying to his face.

As Ant came closer and I stared into his small, insect-like eyes, I realized what a stupid plan it was. I had no chance of pulling it off. Ant would have to be greedier than a drove of starved pigs to believe me.

'I'm listening,' he said, keeping a tight grip on Norman's neck.

I exhaled deeply. Ant must be greedier than every starved pig in the world. He was ready to listen.

'We don't want to fight.' My voice shook with nerves. 'Blood doesn't need to be spilt. The others might want a war, but we don't. I've come to work for you. I have powers.'

'Powers?' Ant asked thoughtfully, his eyes flicking between me, Norman and Bert. 'What powers?'

'I can speak to animals,' I said boldly. 'I can speak Yeti and Werewolf, Wish Frog, Phoenix – I can speak to any rare animal.'

Ant looked down at Norman, who was stooped over, struggling to breathe, as Ant squeezed his neck. 'You hear that, Yeti?' Ant laughed cruelly. 'Sammy has powers. What do you have?'

Norman tried to speak, but only the smallest squeak escaped from his mouth. Ant's fingers tightened their grip and Norman's eyes rolled back in his head and he slumped to the ground.

'Norman!' Bert growled behind me.

OH. MY. GOSH!!!

Ant just killed Norman right in front of me – he squeezed the life right out of him. I tried to stay calm, tried to count to ten in my head. It was a miracle every yeti hiding in the shadows didn't pounce on Ant in a fit of rage.

'So the yeti couldn't fight back, but you think you have powers?' Ant challenged. 'What use is that to me?'

I felt all the blood in my body rush to my face as I struggled to breathe. I lied through my gritted teeth. 'I don't care about Norman. I was only using him to get me and the wish frog here safely. You see, the wish frog can only grant a wish if it has been asked in the official language of Wishing, and I'm the only person alive who can speak it.'

Ant's violet eyes glinted hungrily. I was saying exactly what he wanted to hear – his greed was pulling him further and further into my trap. 'Prove it,' he growled.

'OK. I'm going to wish for Bert to be freed from his chains. Stand back,' I told him, holding my breath and hoping he'd buy it.

Ant gave me the smallest of nods – he was totally buying it.

'OK, now cover your ears. I've noticed that when the Wish Frog grants wishes, it makes the strangest noise. *Release the Yeti Snarl – break Bert free*,' I said in Yeti, hoping that Ant wouldn't know I was speaking Yeti and not Wish Frog.

From the shadows around us came the hum of the deadly Yeti Snarl.

Ant covered his ears and licked his lips with greed as the air around us filled with a deep, deep growl. Ant looked at Bert eagerly, his chest rising and falling as he struggled to control his excitement. The wish frog closed his eyes and opened his mouth wide – is this what he does when he grants wishes?

He raised his front legs into the air as though he was about to conduct an orchestra in a grand symphony.

As the Yeti Snarl vibrated around us, the chains and shackles around Bert's body began to violently shake. There was a sudden groan of metal and then the chains vanished into thin air.

The Yeti Snarl had worked! Bert was free!

'Give him to me,' Ant said, licking his lips at the wish frog and taking a step towards me.

I pulled the wish frog in close to my chest and cupped my hands around him protectively. 'I've already told you – he'll only grant wishes for me.'

'Then you will wish on my behalf,' Ant said, his voice shaking in excitement. 'You will wish that I have an army of ant-like boys, all as strong as me. They will be my loyal worker ants and together we will take over the earth! Wish that I will be king of all – that every person, yeti, beast and shadow will bow down to me! Wish that I will live forever and rule for all eternity!'

This was it, Ant's greed in all its glory. This was his fatal flaw, and his greatest weakness. He was so consumed by greed that he had left himself weak to attack.

'You really are a greedy little weasel,' came Genghis's familiar hiss from the shadows.

The death worm leaped out of nowhere, flying through the air, and lunged at Ant, sinking his dagger-sharp teeth into the scrawny flesh of Ant's arm.

Ant let out a blood-curdling scream and thrashed his arm about in panic. Genghis sunk his teeth in deeper and deeper, spit oozing from his mouth, dripping on to the floor and melting the solid stone ground. Death-worm venom would quickly kill a normal person, but Ant was freakishly strong. However, it seemed to be the antidote to his super-strength.

Genghis's toxic juices pumped further into Ant's veins. Soon Ant grew tired of shaking Genghis's fat body about, and his arm grew limp and weak. 'What are you doing to me?' he cried in panic. 'My strength, it's vanishing!'

Ant fell to the floor. He lifted his head and in the darkness I watched the violet shimmer of his eyes die out and fade to nothing.

There was a gasping for air as Norman twitched and his eyes fluttered open.

'Norman!' I cried. *'You're alive!'*

Sid rushed over to help revive Norman as Jane ran towards Bert and wrapped him in her yeti arms.

All his power taken from him, Ant looked

around in horror. He realized he'd been tricked. As our defeated enemy lay broken on the ground, the yeti army emerged from the shadows.

'What have you done to me? What am I now?' He pleaded with me, and for a moment I almost felt sorry for him. 'Without my strength, I'm nothing.'

The wish frog hopped out of my hand and over towards Ant. He was lying against the wall, grasping his head and fighting back tears.

'Everyone is special,' the wish frog said. 'You don't need powers to be special or to do something remarkable. You should have been happy with the strength you had, and not craved more.'

'Easy for you to say!' Ant cried at the frog. 'You're a wish frog – you can grant any wish you like, have anything you desire.'

'And yet I choose not to,' the frog said calmly. 'I'm happy as I am. You should be too. Your greed got the better of you – it was your downfall.'

Let's get you home, Jane said softly to Bert, leading him away from Ant and out of the cellar. Sid helped Norman to his feet and, together with the yeti army, helped him back up the stairs.

'I'll find a way to get my strength back,' Ant threatened as the successful yeti army lumbered out of the cellar, leaving him alone in the darkness. 'I'll find a way to get my revenge!'

Donny walked up to Ant and threw a calling card at his feet. 'When you realize what you've done, and you want to talk, come and find me. I'm here to help.'

Ant looked at Donny's card in disgust. 'If I ever get my strength back I'll destroy you all!'

'Come near my friends again and I'll be waiting,' spat Genghis.

Ant flinched in fear.

We left Ant alone in the darkness. I felt a bit bad leaving him. 'Surely everyone deserves a second chance,' I said to Donny.

'He needs time to cool off,' Donny answered back. 'Once he's calmed down and he's ready to talk, then he'll call us.'

It was getting light as we clambered back on the bus.

As we pulled away I stared out of the window and watched the mansion slip out of sight. 'Don't feel bad, Sammy,' the wish frog croaked in my ear. 'We've done what we set out to do – we've rescued Bert.'

'Do you think Ant will come after us again?' I asked the frog.

'If he does, we have nothing to worry about.'

I guess he's right – if we can defeat Ant when he's as strong as an army of yetis, then we can beat him again when he has no strength left to boast about.

I was shattered. Tricking Ant and rescuing Bert had exhausted me. I fell asleep to the sound of yeti chatter, with the wish frog sitting in my lap. I stroked his horned little head until we both fell fast asleep.

What a weird, weird day . . .

Monday 27th July

Honestly, I've been too busy to write. Now that Bert has been saved from certain doom and everything in the yeti world is back to normal, you'd think I'd finally have time to kick back and hang out with my friends like everything is normal.

Er, newsflash – nothing is EVER normal!

The day after the successful rescue mission, there was a thorough Ministry of Yetis debrief. I'm happy to report that Norman is back to full health and Bert still has all ten toes – apparently Ant fashioned an impostor yeti toe using sausage meat, yeti fur and Bert's toenail clippings. *'He wasn't as evil as he made out,'* Bert told us. *'He just let his greed get the better of him . . .'*

I'd like to think that we've heard the last of Ant, but that weirdo has had one too many greedyguts smoothies. I don't think he'll be staying quiet for long, super-strength or not!

This turned up in the zoo's post just yesterday:

To EVERYONE at Feral Zoo and beyond,

Don't think this is the last you've heard from me. I'll try every potion, herb and freak cure I can find until I get my strength back. You should be very afraid when I do . . .

Ant

Angry Ant = not great news.

But guess what? Max's death-worm project was a success! He's been offered a place at the Royal College of Zoology so he won't be leaving after all! Grace is beyond happy – she's made up with Max and they're spending every spare minute snogging behind the aviaries again.

Barf x 1,000,000

And that's not the only puke-inducing love affair at Feral Zoo. Jane declared her undying love for Bert and now they're getting married.

'You must come out to Nepal for the wedding,' Bert said to me.

'Thanks for the invitation,' I replied politely. *'But I'm going to the Galapagos Islands with my family tomorrow, sorry.'*

So that's that. We're off to the Galapagos tomorrow. No more zoo, no more yetis, no death worms, Donny or Red for a whole two weeks. My life at Feral Zoo may be C.R.A.Z.Y. but I'm going to miss it while we're away on holiday.

'Are you OK, Sammy?' the wish frog asked as I moped about Backstage.

I nodded. 'I'm pleased to have Bert back,' I said, 'but I'm sad the adventure's over.'

The frog grinned at me and winked cheekily. 'If it wasn't for your brilliant plan, we might never have tricked Ant into freeing Bert. You've done so much to help others, Sammy – you've helped the yetis, Genghis and Max – that someone should help you.'

'What do you mean?' I asked. 'What do I need help with?'

'Anything you like,' he whispered. He lifted his froggy hand and beckoned me closer. I leaned in. 'I want to thank you for all you've done. I want to grant you a wish. You can have anything you like, but you can only wish once. And I won't grant anything until you've thought very long and hard about it.' He sat back on his hind legs looking happy.

I was speechless!

'Me?' I managed. 'Why me? You wouldn't grant Genghis a wish to save Bert.'

The wish frog thought about this for a long moment. 'Wishing is a complicated business. One day I'll explain it to you, Sammy. But I would never have let Bert come to any harm.'

Stop the clocks and let Christmas trees rain down!!!

WOW. WOW. WOW.

If you could have one wish, what would it be?

'Can I think about it?' I asked the wish frog slowly, trying not to faint with excitement.

'I'm not going anywhere, Sammy,' he said

with a grin. 'I like living at Feral Zoo. Take your time, think carefully, and when you work out what you want, come and find me.'

I'm still thinking . . .

Wednesday 5th August

We've been in the Galapagos Islands for over a week now. It's AMAZING here! Penguins, marine iguanas, sea lions – so many cool animals I've lost count!

I've been having way too much fun to keep my diary up to date. I did find time to check my emails this afternoon though, and I found this waiting for me:

Sammy,
Everything at Feral Zoo is as normal as it can be.
The Phoenix hatched anew yesterday – he's so fluffy! The yetis all got off safely and we've nearly got rid of the lingering smell. Genghis is best man

at the wedding, so he's gone back to Nepal too. He's promised to pay us a visit next time he's in town. Is it weird that I miss his sarcastic comments and the sound of him learning English?

I've had a postcard from Bert – he and Jane are back in their Himalayan cave and gearing up for the yeti wedding of the century. They've promised to send us pictures and save us some cabbage cake!

It was so crazy after we rescued Bert that I never got a chance to thank you for everything you did. We really couldn't have done it without you. You're going to make a cracking cryptozoologist one day, Sammy. You'll give me a run for my money!

Take care,
Donny

P.S. Red and the wish frog say hi.

I sat back feeling happy.

Donny was right – with my CSC skills I am going to make a great cryptozoologist. If I can spend the rest of my life helping creatures like

Bert, then I'll be very, very happy. I can't think of a cooler job.

But I don't want to give Donny a 'run for his money' – I don't want to compete. I want to work together.

We're a team, a unit, an army.

Sammy Feral = cryptozoologist-in-training.

Totally weird, and I wouldn't have it any other way.

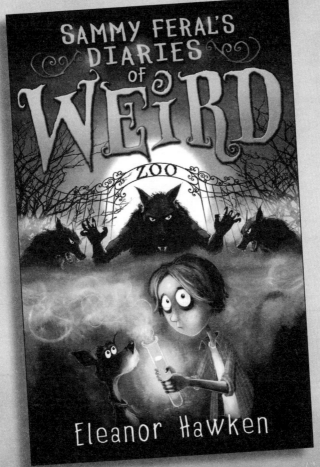

After all the visitors had left I headed towards Dad's office. The plan was to round everyone up and go home for dinner.

But things never, *ever* go to plan.

It was dark outside and the light of a full moon illuminated the animal cages as I walked through the zoo. I could hear barking coming from Dad's office. It sounded like Caliban.

Caliban's growls got louder and louder as I opened the office door. 'Caliban, chill . . .' I started, but I never finished my sentence.

I was way too freaked out by what I saw . . .

As the door swung back I could see Dad sitting behind his desk. Instead of tapping away at his computer, he was staring into space and drooling.

He had bite marks on his neck, huge ones –

it looked as if he'd been bitten by some kind of animal.

'Dad?' I chuckled nervously, hoping he was playing a game.

Dad didn't answer. He made a strange growling sound and curled his lips like an angry dog.

Huh?!

My brain scrambled to understand what was going on.

I took a step closer to Dad's desk, and trod on something soft. I looked down and saw Natty's hand.

My eyes nearly popped out of my head in horror. Mum, Grace and Natty were all lying on the office floor. All as still as stone.

I stopped feeling confused – I felt terrified. Everyone looked dead!

I didn't know whether to puke, laugh or cry – it didn't seem real.

Behind the thumping sound of
my heart I could hear snarling
coming from the corner of
the room.

I looked
up and
saw Caliban
licking his
lips. He paced
towards
me slowly,
reminding
me of a hungry
wolf stalking its
prey. He looked
larger than I remembered and a whole lot more
terrifying.

'Caliban?' I gulped.

Caliban raised his eyes to the ceiling and
let out a mega-loud howl. The sound made

my legs turn to jelly and wobble beneath me.

I had no idea what was happening, but whatever it was I just wanted it to stop. But it didn't stop . . . It just got worse . . .

From the corner of my eye I saw Grace pick herself off the floor. Only she didn't look like Grace – her teeth looked larger, her ears were poking upward from the top of her head and her nose was twitching like mad.

Surely I must be dreaming? None of this could be happening.

Then thick fur started to sprout all over Dad's face . . .

Er, rewind! Face fur?? Yep – face fur!

My brain went into overdrive as I tried to understand what was happening. Was I going nuts? I blinked my eyes like a madman – hoping to wake up from a horrible dream. But I wasn't asleep.

I desperately looked over at Mum. Mum's always great in a crisis – if anyone could put things straight, it was her. But instead of helping me, Mum crouched down on all fours and a tail – that's right, a tail – ripped through her trousers and started to grow out of the base of her back.

Sound crazy? It gets crazier . . .

Natty pulled herself on to her feet like a newborn zombie and let out a howl even louder than Caliban's. Then she dropped on to all fours and looked more like a dog than a six-year-old girl.

My sister was a dog??!!

Without thinking, I inched backwards, ready to run.

Something leaped through the air towards me.

Caliban.

There was a muddy shovel propped against the wall. I reached over and swung it through the air. It skimmed the end of Caliban's nose and he backed away from me.

I thought I'd scared him off. But no – I'd made him MAD!!

Caliban arched his back and growled viciously. He no longer looked like a friendly puppy – he looked like a deadly wolf! Mad rage filled his eyes as he dug his knife-sharp claws into the floor. He slowly put one paw in front of the other as he crept towards me.

I gulped and backed away, into a corner. My back slammed into the wall – there was nowhere else to go . . .

Look out for the next exciting adventure with
SAMMY FERAL

Sammy has to save his best friend Mark from the terrifying curse of the ghostly Hell Hound. Can he defeat the deadly dog in time?